Other Books by Harriet Steel

Becoming Lola
Salvation
City of Dreams
Following the Dream

The Inspector de Silva Mysteries:
Trouble in Nuala
Dark Clouds over Nuala
Offstage in Nuala
Fatal Finds in Nuala
Christmas in Nuala
Passage from Nuala
Rough Time in Nuala
Taken in Nuala

Short stories:
Dancing and other stories

AN INSPECTOR DE SILVA MYSTERY

HIGH WIRE IN NUALA

HARRIET STEEL

Author's Note and Acknowledgements

Welcome to the ninth book in my Inspector de Silva mystery series. Like the earlier ones, this is a self-contained story but, wearing my reader's hat, I usually find that my enjoyment of a series is deepened by reading the books in order and getting to know major characters well. With that in mind, I have included thumbnail sketches of those featuring here who took a major part in previous stories. I have also reprinted this introduction, with apologies to those who have already read it.

Several years ago, I had the great good fortune to visit the island of Sri Lanka, the former Ceylon. I fell in love with the country straight away, awed by its tremendous natural beauty and the charm and friendliness of its people who seem to have recovered extraordinarily well from the tragic civil war between the two main ethnic groups, the Sinhalese and the Tamils. I had been planning to write a detective series for some time and when I came home, I decided to set it in Ceylon in the 1930s, a time when British Colonial rule created interesting contrasts, and sometimes conflicts, with traditional culture. Thus Inspector Shanti de Silva and his friends were born.

I owe many thanks to everyone who helped with this book. My editor, John Hudspith, was, as usual, invaluable, Julia Gibbs did a marvellous job of proofreading the manuscript, and Jane Dixon Smith designed another excellent cover and layout for me. Praise from the many readers who tell me that they have enjoyed previous books in this series and want to know what Inspector de Silva and his friends get up to next encourages me to keep going. Above all, heartfelt thanks go to my husband, Roger for his unfailing encouragement and support, to say nothing of his patience when Inspector de Silva's world distracts me from this one.

Apart from well-known historical figures, all characters in the book are fictitious. Nuala is also fictitious although loosely based on the hill town of Nuwara Eliya. Any mistakes are my own.

Characters who appear regularly in the Inspector de Silva Mysteries

Inspector Shanti de Silva. He began his police career in Ceylon's capital city, Colombo, but, in middle age, he married and accepted a promotion to inspector in charge of the small force in the hill town of Nuala. Likes: a quiet life with his beloved wife, his car, good food, his garden. Dislikes: interference in his work by his British masters; formal occasions.

Sergeant Prasanna. Nearly thirty and married with a daughter. He's doing well in his job and starting to take more responsibility. Likes: cricket and is exceptionally good at it.

Constable Nadar. A few years younger than Prasanna. Diffident at first, he's gaining in confidence. Married with two boys. Likes: his food; making toys for his sons. Dislikes: sleepless nights.

Jane de Silva. She came to Ceylon as a governess to a wealthy colonial family and met and married de Silva a few years later. A no-nonsense lady with a dry sense of humour. Likes: detective novels, cinema, and dancing. Dislikes: snobbishness.

Archie Clutterbuck. Assistant government agent in Nuala and as such, responsible for administration and keeping law and order in the area. Likes: his Labrador, Darcy; fishing; hunting big game. Dislikes: being argued with; the heat.

Florence Clutterbuck. Archie's wife, a stout, forthright lady. Likes: being queen bee; organising other people. Dislikes: people who don't defer to her at all times.

William Petrie. Government agent for the Central Province and therefore Archie Clutterbuck's boss. A charming exterior hides a steely character. Likes: getting things done. Dislikes: inefficiency.

Lady Caroline Petrie. His wife and a titled lady in her own right. She is a charming and gentle person.

Doctor David Hebden. Doctor for the Nuala area. He travelled widely before ending up in Nuala. He's married to Emerald, but they have no children. Under his professional shell, he's rather shy. Likes: cricket. Dislikes: formality.

Emerald Hebden (née Watson). She arrived in Nuala with a touring British theatre company and decided to stay. She's a popular addition to local society. Her full story is told in *Offstage in Nuala*.

Charlie Frobisher. A junior member of staff in the Colonial Service. A personable young man who is tipped to do well. Likes: sport and climbing mountains.

CHAPTER 1

It was a busy Saturday afternoon at Nuala's racecourse, but the crowds had not flocked there to see horse racing, they had come for the Russian circus. Arriving a few days previously, it had aroused a great deal of excitement as the brightly painted wagons carrying the great mounds of canvas for the circus tent and all the other accoutrements that would be required had passed through town on the way to the course.

Posters had gone up in shop windows and on public noticeboards advertising the show. The first performance was taking place that Saturday afternoon. Amongst the promised delights were a high-wire walker, trapeze artists, a dance troupe, jugglers, a fire-eater, and Cossack riders. There was even a snake charmer; an act that de Silva, with his horror of snakes, was dubious he would enjoy. He said as much to Jane as they crossed the racetrack to reach the large area of sandy grass it encircled.

'I'm sure the snake charmer will have his charges well under control. Although I must admit, I was rather surprised to see the act advertised. From what I've read about Russian circuses, snake-charming is not a traditional one, but perhaps this circus puts it on to appeal to audiences from other countries.'

'I thought there might be more animals – elephants say, or lions and tigers. I'm glad to find I was wrong.' De Silva heartily disliked the idea of wild animals being coerced into performing for the entertainment of humans.

'Sadly, in many circuses there would be, but the owners may have thought it too difficult to manage wild animals on long journeys. I believe they're on the road a great deal.'

A little way across the open ground a camp of small tents had been erected, presumably for the circus people to stay in. Beyond it, were a few larger tents that might also be used for accommodation, and then the big top itself. This took pride of place, but many stalls had been set up close to it, like moons around a giant planet. These included a coconut shy, throw-the-ball-in-a-bucket, hoopla, and hook-a-duck. From numerous refreshment stalls there wafted tantalising aromas of spices, coconut, and jaggery, the crumbly, dark-brown sugar that was the staple ingredient of most of the sweetmeats made in Ceylon. De Silva sniffed appreciatively; the smell of jaggery always took him back to his childhood.

Jane put a hand on his arm. 'Shanti, dear, we've only just had lunch.'

He grinned. 'As usual, you read my mind. Perhaps I'll wait until after the show to give in to temptation.'

The crowds milled around; the ladies from the British community wore summery frocks and sunhats, and most of the men were dressed in the cream linen suits and panama hats favoured by Englishmen in the tropics. It was saris for the local ladies, and their menfolk wore tunics of cream or white cotton or linen, smartly trimmed at collar and cuffs, over loose trousers or comfortable sarongs. As it was the weekend, de Silva had chosen the local attire.

Jane surveyed the scene from beneath the wide brim of her straw hat. 'Emerald and David Hebden are over there,' she said. 'Talking with the Applebys. Shall we go and say hello to them?'

'Certainly.'

When they had all exchanged greetings and chatted for a few moments, de Silva looked down at the little girl standing next to Charlotte Appleby. He knew that the Applebys had a large brood of children and guessed this must be one of them; she had her mother's fair hair and blue eyes. He smiled. 'I expect you are almost as excited as I am about watching the circus.'

The little girl held up the toy rabbit she had been cuddling. It was obviously much loved, threadbare in many places with much of its remaining pink fur faded to a greyish white. 'Rabbit's excited too,' she said, smiling shyly back. Everyone laughed.

Raising one hand, George Appleby shielded his eyes from the sun and peered through the crowds.

'Time's getting on. I suppose we ought to round up the rest of the family. The boys went off to play on the stalls. I hope they've made good use of the pocket money I gave them. At least they might get in a bit of bowling practice at the coconut shy.'

'I noticed your eldest up at the club the other day,' remarked David Hebden. 'He's making quite an impression in the under-elevens.'

'Good of you to say so, old chap.'

George Appleby spoke in the offhand tone de Silva had noticed that British men adopted when anyone praised their own, or their family's achievements, but he saw the pleasure in Appleby's eyes. Praise from David Hebden was worth having. He was generally considered to be Nuala's star cricketer.

The Applebys said their goodbyes and disappeared into the crowd.

'Shall we walk around for a little longer?' asked Emerald. 'The performance doesn't start for half an hour, and it might be a bit cooler out here than it will be in the tent with all these people squashed inside.'

'Yes, let's do that,' said Jane.

'There's a stall selling rather pretty straw baskets that I'd like to have a better look at.' Emerald turned to her husband. 'You don't mind, do you, darling?'

David Hebden gave a mock sigh, but he grinned. 'Of course I don't.'

He and de Silva followed in the ladies' wake, chatting easily. Hebden's position as the local doctor brought him into contact with de Silva quite frequently, even before Jane and Emerald had become good friends.

'I don't know much about these circus people,' remarked de Silva. 'I believe they've never visited Nuala before. No doubt that's why their arrival has caused so much excitement.'

'That, and the fact that I think most people are glad of a happy distraction at the moment.'

'You mean the war in Europe?'

'Yes. Early days, of course, and we don't know how it will turn out, but there are plenty who remember the last one. It would be over by Christmas, people said, and it went on for four years.'

Hebden sighed. 'One wonders if mankind will ever learn. Still, mustn't spoil a glorious day. Incidentally, I can tell you something about the circus folk. One of the riggers had an accident when they were in the middle of putting up the tent. Nasty fall, poor chap. He broke his arm, and his boss brought him to the surgery for me to have a look at it. Luckily it was a clean break, so easy enough to set, but he'll have to wear a sling for a few weeks. His boss, who's also the ringmaster, is a fellow called Boris Goncharov. He told me a bit about his company while I was patching up his employee. Most of his people are Russian as he is, but they've been travelling all over the East for years. Goncharov said they left Russia in the early '20s when things started to look not so good for them. I assume their way of life didn't fit into the communist scheme of things.'

From what de Silva remembered hearing of the tightening of the grip of the communist state in the years following the Russian Revolution, he imagined that leaving had been a wise decision, but he felt extremely sorry for anyone who was forced to turn their back on their homeland.

They caught up with Jane and Emerald who were debating the merits of two straw bags: one in natural straw and the other dyed pink. 'The plain one will be stronger and carry more,' remarked Jane, holding it up.

'But the pink one is prettier.' Emerald turned to the stallholder, who waited for a decision with a patient smile on his chubby face. 'The pink is a very good choice, memsahib,' he said. 'It goes with your dress.'

'Then that settles it,' said Emerald briskly.

A few moments of bargaining ensued until both parties felt that honour had been satisfied.

'I suggest we go and find seats before all the good ones are gone,' said Hebden. 'It's bound to be full. They're not giving any evening performances and they're only here a few days.'

The sides of the tent around the area where the audience were to sit had been rolled up and the air inside was less stuffy than de Silva had feared it would be. The heat was, however, bound to increase as more people crowded in. Jane and Emerald had brought fans, but he and Hebden would simply have to endure any discomfort.

Moving slowly down a side aisle, they found themselves behind Reverend Peters and his wife. De Silva was surprised to see them; he wouldn't have associated the dry, albeit very pleasant, vicar of Nuala's Anglican church with an entertainment as frivolous as a circus. Perhaps Peters had come to please his wife. Mrs Peters beamed as she talked to Emerald and Jane and was clearly enjoying herself, but in the hubbub de Silva was unable to hear what was being said. She was a small lady with a waif-like figure, who looked even smaller when seen beside her lanky husband. She wore her grey hair scraped into a bun at the nape of her neck, but the severity of the hairstyle was mitigated by the habitually kind expression on her homely face. Like a baked apple, there was something wholesome about her.

'You were having a long chat with the vicar's wife,' he observed to Jane as he slid into the seat beside her when they and the Hebdens had found room a few rows back and on the opposite side of the aisle from where the Peters had taken their seats.

'She was telling me about the circuses she remembers watching as a girl. She's a real enthusiast.'

'I can't believe her husband is.'

'I was surprised too, but apparently he was eager to come. I knew he has a great interest in orchids, but I had no idea that he's also a keen ophiologist.'

'A what?'

'Snakes, dear. He's interested in snakes.'

'Good grief. Whatever for? All I want to know about snakes is that they are a long way from wherever I am. As I said, I'm already worried about this snake charmer.'

She squeezed his hand. 'And as I've told you, I'm sure you've no need to be concerned.' She glanced in the Peters' direction. 'Apparently, this isn't Reverend Peters' first visit here. He came up the day before yesterday on the pretext of introducing himself and inviting anyone who was interested to come to church tomorrow, but according to his wife, what he really wanted to do was buttonhole this snake charmer and talk to him about snakes.'

'Did he succeed?'

'Oh, yes. Mrs Peters said the man was delighted to meet a fellow enthusiast, and the vicar came home very pleased with his excursion. He was gone for hours. It seems the snake charmer has numerous snakes that he doesn't use in his act, as well as those that he does, so they had plenty to talk about.'

De Silva looked around him. 'I see that Archie and Florence Clutterbuck have brought a party from the Residence.'

He recognised quite a few of the assistant government agent's staff, but sadly Charlie Frobisher, with whom he usually had the most to do, was absent. He had come to the police station not long ago to say goodbye. He had enlisted in the Royal Air Force and was going up to the base at China Bay in the north of the island to train as a pilot. De Silva remembered David Hebden's remarks about the war, and a shiver went through him. He hoped Frobisher would come through unscathed.

'Prasanna and Kuveni, and Nadar and his wife are over there,' Jane remarked. 'With the children.'

'Where? Oh yes, I see.' De Silva raised a hand to greet his sergeant and his constable, but as they were busy keeping their excited children in their seats, he doubted they noticed him.

'Prasanna and Kuveni's little girl's grown such a lot since I last saw her,' said Jane. 'But then young children do grow fast. It makes me feel old.'

He squeezed her hand. 'But still beautiful. And not old,' he added hastily.

Jane giggled. 'Gracious, if this is the effect the circus has on you, we should come every day it's here.'

A small band consisting of three trumpeters, two cymbal players, an accordionist, and two drummers was positioned at one side of the brightly lit ring. Suddenly, the trumpeters raised their instruments to their lips and a loud fanfare broke through the buzz of conversation. Jane leant forward in her seat. 'I think they're about to begin. How exciting!'

The audience fell silent as a tall, bull-chested man dressed in black trousers, a black cutaway coat, a scarlet waistcoat and bow tie, and a crisp, dazzlingly white shirt strode into the centre of the ring. The light from the electric bulbs that were strung in scallops around the ring accentuated the glossy sheen of his black top hat, and the gold finial of his ringmaster's baton sparkled. A deeply fringed white scarf that draped with the suppleness of silk added a touch of suave informality to the outfit. Presumably this was Boris Goncharov, the man Hebden had met. He certainly cut an impressive figure. His moustache was artfully tweaked up at the ends, and his beard clipped to a point, giving him a slightly satanic air. When he doffed his hat to the audience, de Silva saw that his dark hair was slicked down in the style made fashionable by the stars he and Jane saw in the Hollywood films shown at Nuala's Gaiety Cinema.

A drum roll silenced the last murmurs of conversation. Boris raised his baton then brought it down smartly on the ground, raising a little puff of sawdust. 'Ladies and gentlemen!' He smiled, gesturing to the children in the front row. 'And our young friends! Welcome!'

As he continued to talk, extolling the talents of the performers they were about to see, de Silva gradually became accustomed to his accent. In contrast to the clipped way the British spoke it, the English language rolled off his tongue like warmed treacle. 'And now,' he concluded. 'I have spoken enough. It is time we entertain you.' The rich bass voice rose to a volume that de Silva was surprised it still had in reserve. 'Are you ready?'

There were muffled sounds of assent.

An exaggerated frown on his face, Boris cupped a hand to his ear. 'I do not hear you!'

Laughter and shouts of "ready!" rose from the audience, but he carried on pretending not to hear them until almost all the adults had joined in and the children were squealing with excitement. At last, he made a sweeping gesture that encompassed the members of the band. 'Music!'

The first act was the dance troupe that had been advertised on the posters. To the parp of trumpets, the clash of cymbals, and the beat of drums, they performed an energetic, whirling dance that made de Silva feel quite giddy just watching it. The men wore black trousers cinched in below their knees to form pantaloons; their loose white shirts, decorated with scarlet, yellow, and green ribbons billowed as they gyrated. The women's costumes, made of vividly coloured fabric, were more elaborate. The skirts were full and cut just above the ankle, ballooning as their wearers danced. Tightly fitted over diaphanous white blouses with full sleeves, they were complemented by embroidered waistcoats. The men were bareheaded, but the women sported flowers and wreaths of greenery in their dark hair.

When the dancing ended, two clowns came on. Both were men, dressed in baggy, multi-coloured check trousers and tunics. Greasepaint whitened their faces, and their exaggerated, scarlet lips clashed with their orange wigs. De Silva wondered if there was such a thing as a female clown. Certainly, the outfits were far from flattering, so perhaps it wasn't a role that appealed to women.

The taller of the clowns snatched up a tin bucket and began to run around the front of the ring, scooping out handfuls of red, orange, and blue confetti and throwing them into the audience. Finally, to loud laughter and applause, he upended the bucket over the head of a stout, balding man in the front row. What remained of the bucket's contents rained down on the man's head, which brought even more laughter from the crowd. De Silva guessed he was a Britisher and wondered whether he would be amused by the clown's antics, but fortunately, when he stood up, turning slightly as he brushed confetti from his clothes, he seemed to be laughing as heartily as his companions.

Meanwhile, the other clown had fetched a wooden ladder. He made a great business of looking for his friend, swinging the ladder as he swirled around. The taller clown had dropped the bucket and now scampered around the ring, making sure that the clown with the ladder always had his back to him. Shouts of "He's behind you!" rose from the audience, but the clown with the ladder just scratched his head, shrugged his shoulders, and carried on turning around. Finally, a particularly energetic swing of the ladder almost knocked the taller clown over, but just in time, he ducked. The shorter clown jabbed the ladder at him and, to the accompaniment of gales of laughter, a comical race around the ring began. De Silva's ribs ached. The clowns' antics were silly, but very entertaining. He wondered how the act would end.

At last the clown with the ladder, who was now the pursued rather than the pursuer, propped it against one of the tent poles and started to scramble up the rungs. The taller clown stopped; with a gleeful grin on his face, he mimed a question to the audience: should he push the ladder over? There was more laughter and hoots of encouragement. The shorter clown clung on as the ladder tilted slowly backwards then, just at the moment when it seemed impossible for him to keep his balance any longer, he swung sideways and dived towards the sawdust-covered ground, curling into a forward roll as he landed. He lay still for a moment while the audience clapped vigorously then jumped to his feet. Joining hands, he and the other clown took their bows and bounded off into the wings. De Silva was mightily amused.

The acts rolled on: first, a quartet of flying acrobats. Graceful as swallows and lithe as eels, they dazzled the audience with their daring feats of athleticism and speed. Next came a juggler, then a knife thrower, and after that more dancing, and the promised fire-eater. When the snake charmer appeared, de Silva was surprised that he managed to forget some of his fears in the fascination of watching the man. Compared to Boris, he had a slight, sinewy frame. He wore his thick, lustrous black hair long and curling at the neck, and his complexion was dark. De Silva decided that he must be a local, or perhaps an Indian, rather than a Russian.

Each of the two large straw baskets he brought on turned out to contain two snakes. Sitting cross-legged on the ground, the snake charmer coaxed them out. De Silva shuddered as they slithered across the sawdust then halted, rearing up in front of their master and waving their heads in time with the music that he made. To de Silva, the instrument looked very like the Indian *magudi*. It was a long wooden pipe with a gourd-shaped bowl at one end, decorated with woollen cords and braid. Even to the human ear, the tunes the snake charmer drew from it were hypnotic.

All except one of the snakes was about the length of a man's arm and as thick, but the fourth was a little shorter and thinner. From the shape and carriage of its head, de Silva guessed it was a young cobra, but he didn't recognise the others. One had scales of a rich, glossy brown and the others were olive green. He supposed they were fine specimens, but since the mere sight of them made his skin crawl, he found true admiration impossible.

The snake charmer played on for a while as the snakes continued to perform their swaying dance, then he put down his instrument and stood up. De Silva watched in horror as he grasped the young cobra by the nape of its neck and put it back in one of the baskets. The olive-green pair followed and when he had stowed them, he picked up the brown snake. As casually as if it were a scarf, he wound it around his neck then let it crawl down his arm. When it reached his wrist, he took hold of it again and wrapped it around his waist before drawing it into yet more contortions.

To de Silva, this part of the act seemed to last for a very long time. He alternated between frozen respect for the snake charmer's courage and heart-stopping fear that something would go wrong. He imagined the snake striking out and then escaping into the audience. His fear increased when the snake charmer put the brown snake back in its basket and took out one of the olive-green ones again. Smiling, he strolled over to the front row of the audience and walked along it. Many people recoiled as he passed; finally, he picked out a lanky young man with ginger hair.

The audience clapped as the young man stood up and left his seat, following the snake charmer into the ring. To de Silva's amazement, he appeared to remain calm while the olive-green snake crawled up his leg, over his torso and around his neck, its forked tongue flicking, and its head swaying gently from side to side. When the snake charmer brought this part of the act to a close, taking back his snake, de Silva realised that he had been holding his breath for a long time. The ginger-haired man shook hands with the snake charmer and returned to his seat to great applause.

'I could never do what he's just done,' de Silva muttered to Jane.

She smiled and patted his hand. 'Do you want to?'

'Goodness, no.'

'Then let's hope it's never necessary.'

The snake charmer left the ring, taking his reptilian charges with him, and Boris Goncharov strode on again.

'Please forgive us, ladies and gentlemen. Today, sadly, we have no horses to entertain you. The journey here was long, and they are enjoying a well-deserved rest. You must come back tomorrow. However, ladies and gentlemen, we do have for you—' He paused, smiling broadly and displaying remarkably white teeth. 'An incredible young lady, who is famous from the steppes of Mother Russia to the shores of your Indian Ocean.'

Drums rolled and the audience waited expectantly. Moving off to one side of the entrance to the ring, Boris doffed his top hat. 'Ladies and gentlemen! Please welcome, our dazzling star – Tatiana!'

Truly, the young woman who sashayed on was a dazzling sight. Her raven hair was braided and coiled around a delicately shaped head, the style accentuating a lovely face with sparkling, dark eyes, and a flawless complexion. She moved as lightly as a petal falling from one of the roses in de Silva's garden. Her ballet tutu was a splash of scarlet that glittered as it caught the light. It showed off her boyish figure to perfection.

'She must be the high-wire walker,' whispered Jane. 'There was a picture of her on the poster.'

De Silva's stomach lurched as he glanced up to where the high wire sliced through thin air, attached at each end to the tops of two flimsy-looking wooden towers. Close to the one on the left a trapeze dangled, ready for use. He noticed that the trapeze on the right, which the quartet of flying acrobats had used in their show, had been pulled back out of sight.

As the first wave of applause subsided, a woman who looked several years older than Tatiana followed her into the ring. Boris raised a hand to quieten the audience. 'And now, her partner, Izabella.' The way he spoke the name gave it a sibilant emphasis that reminded de Silva of a snake.

Izabella was taller than Tatiana and far less striking. Her narrow face looked pinched, and her smile was brittle. She too wore her dark hair braided and coiled, but her eyes lacked sparkle. Although an attempt had obviously been made to enliven her complexion by the application of carmine to her lips and cheeks, it was sallow.

'I wonder what part she takes,' remarked Jane. 'The poster only showed Tatiana. Izabella looks strong, doesn't she? Maybe there will be times when Tatiana needs her.'

'I suppose so,' de Silva replied absently. He had to admit, he was having trouble taking his eyes off Tatiana, as he imagined were many of the men in the audience. She was now climbing gracefully to the top of the left-hand tower, followed by Izabella. When she came level with the trapeze she reached out and pulled it towards her, then with practised ease, swung across to sit on it. Beginning to swing back and forth, she slipped into a graceful series of balletic moves, sometimes perched on the trapeze, sometimes hanging from it with only her bent knees to stop her falling. Gasps of apprehension, and rounds of clapping when danger was past, evidenced the audience's appreciation.

After a while she reached out and pulled herself back to the tower where Izabella waited, and they changed places for her part of the act. This relied more on strength than grace and pleased the audience in its own way. As it neared the end, de Silva noticed that a short piece of rope with a metal bar at the bottom hung off the trapeze. His throat tightened as Izabella took the bar between her teeth, let go of the trapeze itself and propelled herself into a vertiginous spin.

'She was exceptionally good too,' observed Jane when, with Izabella safely back on the tower, the audience applauded enthusiastically. 'Not as graceful, as Tatiana, but one sees why strength was needed. I hope Tatiana will do her high-wire act now.'

As Tatiana returned, de Silva wondered why she, as well as Izabella, had performed on the trapeze. It seemed to him that the high-wire act would be enough on its own, for it must require a great deal of concentration. The sound of clapping faded as she stepped onto the high wire and took the long pole that Izabella held out to her. De Silva winced and closed his eyes. When he opened them, she had already walked several feet along the wire, holding the pole at chest height to aid her balance. Gracefully, she continued towards the tower on the opposite side, for all the world as if she were taking a leisurely stroll in the countryside.

So tense that you could almost touch it, a hush had fallen over the audience. The low, pulsing beat of the drums heightened the apprehension that filled the air. Every time Tatiana paused, there were gasps of alarm. A pain throbbed behind de Silva's eyes. He felt as if he was making the slow walk with her. At last, the end of the wire was not far away. Tatiana turned her head a fraction towards the audience; he glimpsed a smile of mischievous triumph on her face. She took another step closer to the tower, and the audience exhaled a collective sigh of relief. Soon she would be safe. Clapping began to swell.

And then it died.

She had only a few more steps to take to reach the tower, but something was wrong. Her left foot came down next then slipped off the wire. She swayed and tried to put her weight on the right one, but that too slid away from under her. Dropping the pole, she launched herself at the wooden tower, her outstretched hands clawing frantically for something to cling on to. It seemed that minutes passed, although they were probably only seconds, before she fell. As she plummeted towards the sawdust-covered ring, the pole hit the ground and bounced away; she landed with a sickening thud and to screams from the audience that had de Silva's heart racing.

With surprising speed for such a big man, the ringmaster, Boris, was beside Tatiana's inert body. He dropped to his knees and tried to rouse her as several of the circus hands rushed to join him, screening the scene from the audience. A stretcher was produced, and she was carried away.

Boris stumbled to his feet and faced the audience. 'Ladies and gentlemen! Do not be alarmed. But if there is a doctor here, please come forward.'

Jane put her hand to her throat. 'Gracious, if she's not badly hurt, she'll be a fortunate young lady. She fell a long way and with only the sawdust to cushion her fall.'

Grimly, de Silva suspected that Boris was merely trying to reassure the audience.

David Hebden was already on his feet. He paused briefly as he squeezed past de Silva's drawn-up knees and they exchanged glances. De Silva saw that his friend was as dubious as he was about Boris's words.

The ring had emptied and the dance troupe that had opened the proceedings returned. This time, they were dressed in oriental costume, glittering with jewellery of such barbaric splendour that it must, thought de Silva, be imitation. But despite all their efforts, they failed to hold the audience's attention. The musicians too played with a will, their faces red and shiny with exertion, but their eyes strayed to the exit where Tatiana had been carried away.

'They might do better to stop,' muttered Jane.

'I agree,' said Emerald. 'That poor girl. I hope her injuries aren't serious.'

Privately, de Silva thought that was extremely unlikely.

At last, the dancers abandoned their increasingly fruitless quest to keep the audience entertained and melted away into the wings. The ringmaster, Boris, reappeared. This time, he had removed his hat and his broad face was solemn. Even at a distance, de Silva saw how he struggled to control his feelings.

'Ladies and gentlemen. Please forgive us. For today, we must end.' He gestured to the grassy area outside. 'But the sun shines. Please, eat, drink.' He forced a smile. 'Another day, the show goes on.'

* * *

'Oh how sad,' said Jane as they gathered themselves together and started to move slowly along the row towards the aisle. 'What a pity that such a lovely day had to end this way.'

'It's hard to understand what went wrong,' remarked

Emerald, looking puzzled. 'Surely that high wire is checked before it's used, but there seemed to be some kind of problem. Something that made her lose her balance. Unless her concentration failed her, but that's hard to credit. She looked so composed until then, and if it was a loss of concentration, why at the last moment when she was so nearly home?'

De Silva recalled that smile of triumph. Why indeed? Had Tatiana made the grave error of relaxing a moment too soon? It was something that he was aware he needed to guard against in his own work.

He heard a familiar voice call his name and looked round to see Archie Clutterbuck shouldering his way through the crowd towards them. The press of moving people made it impossible to stop, but he had nearly caught up with them by the time they stepped out of the tent, allowing them to pause as the crowd thinned and there was more room for manoeuvre. Leaving Jane and Emerald standing in a nearby patch of shade, de Silva waited for him.

'Good afternoon, sir.'

'Afternoon, de Silva. Terrible accident, eh? All most unfortunate. Just when the afternoon was going so well.'

'Indeed it is, sir. And I'd be surprised if the lady's injuries are not worse than the ringmaster's saying.'

'So would I, de Silva. So would I. I saw Hebden take himself off to help.'

'I think I'll go round there too. Just in case there's anything I can do. Doctor Hebden may appreciate some support.'

Archie rubbed his chin. 'In my opinion, as these people aren't British, it's not really a matter for us. But I know you, de Silva. Belt and braces, eh? Well, if you're going, I may as well come with you. Show the flag and all that. On reflection, there are people here who'd probably expect me to.'

'Of course, sir.'

'What about your wife and Mrs Hebden? Do they have any way of getting home by themselves? If they need transport, I'm sure we can find room in one of our cars.'

'That would be kind.'

Archie beckoned to a servant who hovered close by. 'Go and make sure one of the cars waits for the two ladies over there, then come back and escort them to the car park.'

The servant gave a little bow and hurried off.

Having explained the plan to Jane and Emerald, de Silva and Archie set off into the tent once more.

CHAPTER 2

Away from the ring there was no electric lighting, and later oil lamps would be lit, but for now enough daylight penetrated for de Silva and Archie to see by. They followed the sound of voices until they came to a short corridor with an exit to the outside and a large, tented room at the far end. From the props and items of clothing lying around on benches and chairs, de Silva guessed that it was the place where the circus members assembled while they waited to go into the ring.

Tatiana had been placed on a table at the far side of the room. Several people stood around her including Hebden and Boris Goncharov, who had discarded his top hat and silk scarf. Both men's expressions were grave. Deep in conversation, they didn't notice the new arrivals until Hebden looked up and came over to them.

'It's not good news, I fear,' he said. 'She would have been very lucky to survive a fall like that.'

Archie frowned. 'Do you mean the poor girl's dead?'

'I'm afraid so. In the circumstances, it may be a blessing. If she had survived, it would have been with terrible, life-changing injuries.' He looked back at Tatiana's body and the woebegone group of people stood around it. 'Tragic. Apparently, she was barely twenty.'

'I'd better go over and talk to whoever's in charge,' said Archie. 'That ringmaster fellow, I assume. I ought to convey our official sympathies.'

'His name is Boris Goncharov.'

'Was the young lady related to any of the people here?'

'I'm not sure.'

As Hebden and Archie went over to the table where Tatiana's body lay, de Silva heard a movement behind him. He hung back for a moment and, turning, saw one of the clowns. He might know something about the girl's family. De Silva put a hand on his arm to detain him.

'Do you speak English?'

The clown nodded. 'Some.'

'Then I'd like a word with you. I am Inspector de Silva of the Nuala police,' he added.

The clown still wore his costume and makeup but had removed the orange wig. It had concealed a sweat-sheened head that, apart from a few strands of damp grey hair plastered across it, was bald as an egg. Now, his kohl-pencilled eyes and scarlet mouth gave him a grotesque rather than a comedic air.

'Tatiana Petrovna had no relation. How do you say? Of her blood?' he replied when de Silva asked the question. 'But she grow up in Goncharov family with Boris, and Alexei Ivanovich.'

'Alexei?'

'Young brother of Boris Ivanovich.'

'Boris Ivanovich?' De Silva was puzzled. 'Isn't the family name Goncharov?'

The clown nodded. 'Yes, but it is, what do you say, polite for me to call him this. You understand?'

De Silva didn't fully, but he let it pass. Probably Jane would know the reason for the change of name.

'Is this Alexei with the circus too?'

The clown made a sound somewhere between a grunt and a laugh. 'He own half.'

De Silva frowned. 'Is there a problem with that?'

'Big problem,' said the clown, rolling his eyes.

'Where's this Alexei now? Doesn't he perform?'

The clown nodded. 'He look after the horses and does show with three other riders, but today, no show.'

De Silva recalled Boris mentioning that the horses were weary from the journey and were being rested.

'Alexei Ivanovich say two horses are lame. Boris Ivanovich say this not his fault. Make shorter act with two well horses.' The clown shrugged. 'They argue. It is nothing new. Alexei Ivanovich, he does not give in. Now for sure Boris Ivanovich will say Tatiana Petrovna's accident is because of this. She make her act too long and this why she make mistake.'

De Silva wondered why Tatiana should be the one to change her act. He was about to ask the clown when he saw Hebden beckon him over. He thanked the clown and asked his name in case he wanted to find him again.

'Gordo. My name is Gordo,' the clown replied.

Over in the group, Boris was speaking forcefully to a man de Silva recognised as one of the lead dancers. He looked older than the other men there. They spoke in a language that de Silva presumed was Russian.

'What's going on?' he asked Hebden quietly.

'Goncharov's trying to find out where his brother, Alexei, is. No one seems to know. Do you have any idea where Emerald has got to?'

'Archie offered her and Jane a seat in one of the Residence's cars. I expect they'll be on the way home by now.'

'I'll have a word and thank him, then I want to nip home and make sure all this hasn't upset her. If you like, I'll have a word with the manager of the undertakers too. Their office won't be open over the weekend, but I have his home telephone number. In this heat, we ought to remove the poor girl's body as soon as possible.'

'I agree. Thank you.'

'I'll be back shortly in case there's anything else I can do.'

As Hebden walked away to speak to Archie, who was standing a little apart from the group and observing the proceedings, a man who de Silva recognised as the snake charmer made some remark to Boris. With a dismissive gesture, he shrugged before speaking again to the lead dancer. It was impossible for de Silva to understand the words, but he guessed Boris was telling him to go and look for Alexei, for soon he and his companions left the tent. The snake charmer followed them.

Boris turned his attention to de Silva. 'Who are you?' he asked abruptly. De Silva bridled then remembered he was not in uniform.

'My name is Inspector de Silva of the Nuala police.'

Hebden had now left, and Archie joined them.

'Ah, good. You've introduced yourselves,' he said briskly. He turned to Boris. 'I must be getting along now. I'll leave you in my inspector's capable hands. I imagine he may have a few questions for you. Once again, please accept my condolences and those of His Majesty's government. De Silva, a moment before I go, please.'

Leaving Boris alone with Tatiana's body, Archie drew de Silva aside. 'The poor fellow's in pretty bad shape,' he said in an undertone, although Boris didn't appear to be listening. 'I suggest you keep your questions to the minimum, but as it's on our patch, so to speak, I suppose you ought to file a report of the accident.' He glanced back at Boris who remained with Tatiana's body, apparently lost in thought. 'No need to make a meal of it though,' he added. 'As I said, these people are not British, and in any case, they're only due to stay on here for a few days. You might give me a call later. Just so that I have a bit more information if anyone asks. Otherwise, do your best to be discreet.'

De Silva nodded. Obviously, Archie didn't want to put

himself out, but on the other hand, he probably wouldn't like any of the British community who happened to ask him about the affair to think that he had simply hurried home for tea. Or more probably – by the time Archie reached the Residence – a whisky and soda.

Left alone with Boris, de Silva saw that his shoulders slumped, and he was wiping his cheeks with a handkerchief. His bow tie hung unfastened and he had unbuttoned the collar of his shirt. Its crisp material was now limp and stained with patches of sweat; black hairs curled from the open neck. Revealing itself to be no more than a prop, the upturned moustache was gone. De Silva felt a stab of pity.

'I'll do my best to keep things brief, sir,' he said. 'But I hope you understand that in a case like this, I need to record details of the accident. I may also need to question a few people and take down statements.'

Boris looked at him dully. 'I understand.'

'I believe that you and the young lady were not related by blood but did have a family connection.'

'Who told you this?'

'One of your clowns. He said his name was Gordo.'

'Ah,' Boris said listlessly. 'What else did he tell you?'

The poor man had enough to cope with without discussing his family difficulties. De Silva decided not to divulge what the clown had told him about the relationship between Boris and his brother. Fortunately, the ringmaster didn't wait for an answer.

'It will be hard for the circus to recover,' he said sadly. 'We all loved Tatiana.' He spread his hands in a gesture of despair. 'To replace her also – I do not know how we can do it.' He sighed. 'There will be other problems. My people will be afraid. They believe a death in the circus brings bad luck.'

'I'd like to speak to whoever rigged up the high wire and trapeze. From my position in the audience, it appeared that the young lady encountered an unexpected hazard at the end of the wire.'

Boris's gaze lingered on Tatiana's body. From his expression, de Silva deduced that he was unwilling to leave her.

'Perhaps someone else can show me the way,' he said gently.

Boris seemed to consider this for a moment then sighed. 'No, I take you. I must be with you when you talk with my people. Most of them speak only Russian.'

* * *

Three circus hands sat in the shade of a tree some way off from the rear entrance to the main tent. Two of them looked up with abject expressions on their faces, but the eldest man's expression was defiant. He acted as spokesmen for the other two as Boris relayed de Silva's questions.

'He say everything was done properly,' Boris explained. 'Tatiana has made checks as usual. Izabella too.'

De Silva was not surprised. He imagined that anyone taking the risks that they did would want to satisfy themselves all was in order, not rely on others to do so. So, what had gone wrong? He would have to try another approach.

'I'd like the wire lowered,' he said. 'I think a closer inspection needs to be made. Please get your men to do that.'

'It will take time, but we can do it.'

Boris barked something in Russian, and the three circus hands headed back in the direction of the tent.

'I understand from Gordo that you own the circus together with your brother,' said de Silva as they followed them.

Boris grunted. 'Yes. I have sent men to find him and tell him what has happened.' He seemed oddly unconcerned by his brother's absence, but de Silva didn't pursue it.

By the time they reached the ring, the two younger circus hands were already climbing the towers while the eldest one stood below, shouting up orders. Boris went to sit alone, and de Siva left him in peace. Apart from the sound of the circus hands climbing the tower, it was eerily quiet. Hard to believe that the tent had been filled with laughter and applause only an hour or two earlier. De Silva stirred the sawdust at his feet with the toe of his shoe and smelled the tangy aroma of resin.

Someone had extinguished all but a few of the electric lights and rolled down most of the canvas sides behind where the audience had sat. Shadows crept over the banks of seating. A vision of rows of ghostly faces murmuring a lament rose before de Silva's eyes. With an involuntary shiver, he recalled what Boris had said about the belief that a death in the circus brought bad luck. It was something he must bear in mind. It was not only circus folk who believed in bad luck. He didn't want rumours to get around town, and stories to become distorted. The circus had been welcomed, but that might change.

A quiet step and a low cough drew his attention from the circus hands' progress.

'How's it going?' asked David Hebden.

'These three are the men who rigged up the high wire. They insist – at the least the eldest one does, the others don't say much – that everything was done properly. Tatiana and Izabella checked everything too.'

'It's unlikely there was anything wrong with the tensioning of the wire then.'

'It looks that way. One of the clowns I spoke to told me the act was longer than usual, so it's possible Tatiana's concentration wavered, but I'm not convinced that's all there was to it. I think there was a problem at the end of the wire too. Something that made her lose her balance. She seemed too skilled to make a mistake unless there was a contributory factor.'

The two circus hands were descending the towers now, lowering the wire between them as they went.

'Well, now's our chance to find out,' said Hebden as they reached the ground and laid the wire out on the sawdust.

Going over to it, de Silva found that it was composed of lengths of steel, tightly woven to give it strength. He followed Hebden along the line of it, only making a cursory inspection of the left-hand side and the centre; if necessary, they could be checked again. Hebden reached the end and knelt down in the sawdust. 'There's something here. Come and have a look, de Silva.'

Unlike the rest of the wire which had been quite shiny, the section Tatiana had fallen from had a dull, milky sheen to it. Hebden ran a finger along it then showed the fingertip to de Silva.

'There's something greasy here. Only a trace, but it seems odd.' He stood up. 'I suggest we go back to that room and see if there's any on the lady's footwear. It might explain why she got into difficulties.'

Back in the tented room, Hebden folded back part of the sheet that covered Tatiana, exposing her feet. In turn, he lifted each one carefully and examined her pink satin ballet pumps. 'The soles are stained. Maybe just from wear but,' he prodded one gently, 'there might be more to it than that.'

De Silva peered over his shoulder. 'May I touch?'

'Be my guest.'

De Silva felt a vestige of grease. He leaned closer and sniffed the soft leather. The woody odour of sawdust was mingled with a greasy smell. It was possible that Tatiana had picked up something on her feet before she climbed onto the wire, but it was strange that she had walked almost to the end before it caused her any difficulty.

'I wonder if that circus chap was hiding something,' said Hebden with a frown. 'Why would there be grease on the wire when the last thing anyone would want would be for it to be slippery? Perhaps one of the circus hands had been using some on it and not wiped it away carefully enough.'

'But why would that be necessary in the first place?'

Hebden shrugged. 'Only trying to think of an explanation, de Silva. My father was an engineer. Lubrication seemed to play an important part in all kinds of operations. Maybe there was a kink in the weave of the wire, or some such thing, that needed easing back into place.'

It was an inventive idea, but de Silva was not convinced.

'We may as well go back to the ring,' said Hebden. 'It might be worth having another word with our friend Boris. Get him to ask his people a few more questions.'

Boris sat in one of the front row seats, staring at the ground. De Silva was about to go and speak to him, but at that moment the ringmaster stirred and stood up. He walked over to them. 'You find something?' he asked wearily.

When de Silva showed him the suspicious section of wire, he frowned. 'What is this?' He shouted for the circus hands who shambled over with a show of reluctance. From the words exchanged, de Silva guessed that they were denying all knowledge.

'They say they know nothing about it,' said Boris when the exchange finished. 'They did not put anything on wire. It was not needed, and if they had, they clean it away.'

The eldest circus hand spoke again, apparently issuing an even more forceful denial than before. De Silva decided he was probably telling the truth. It wouldn't be worth his job to make a mistake.

'I'm afraid I must be off and leave you to deal with this, de Silva,' said Hebden. 'I need to pack for a trip that I'm going on tomorrow morning. Some old chums from my Kandy days have arranged a fishing trip and asked me to come with them.'

'I won't hold you up then. Thank you for your help.'

'Think nothing of it.'

As Hebden walked away across the sawdust-strewn ring and disappeared through one of the public exits into the sunshine, de Silva debated what he should do next. If someone had tampered with the wire, he must find out who they were. They would have to be sufficiently fit to climb up the tower. Would they also need to be skilled enough to step along the wire to the spot where it was greasy? Maybe so, but how would they be able to lean down to apply a substance and still maintain their balance? Could they have had something like a long-handled brush or mop and leant off the tower to apply it from there? Swiftly, he ran over the possibilities and came up with Tatiana's partner, Izabella, as a prime suspect. She obviously had a head for heights. The flying acrobats must have too, but on the facts that he had established so far, Izabella was more involved with Tatiana than they were.

'You have more questions?' asked Boris.

'I'd like a word with Tatiana's partner, Izabella.'

Boris said something to the circus hands and one of the younger ones went away. When Boris turned back to de Silva, his expression was troubled.

'You think Izabella know something?' he asked.

'I'm not sure, but I need to question her. How long has she worked with Tatiana for?'

'Two years.'

'And who had the most experience?'

'Izabella, by much. This is why I want them to work together. Tatiana—' There was a catch in his voice. 'Sometimes too confident.'

So Izabella had more experience but was not presented as the star of the show. De Silva wondered how she felt about that.

'Is she too from Russia?'

'No, Izabella Rabach is Hungarian. She joined in Malaya. The circus she worked in had some problems.' He frowned. 'She is difficult woman, but I don't believe she is bad one.'

'Nevertheless, I must question her.'

'Of course.'

'Does she speak any English?'

'Only a little, but I will translate.'

They waited in silence for Izabella to be brought. De Silva noticed there were beads of sweat on Boris's face. The effects of repressed anxiety and grief as much as of the temperature, he imagined. Briefly, it crossed his mind that there had still, as far as he knew, been no news of the whereabouts of Boris's brother, Alexei. Surely, the search party would have found him by now; the Nuala racetrack was not that large a place. It was odd that he had not come to grieve with his brother, and if he knew de Silva was there – and he had made no secret of it – to talk to the police. Sadly, it indicated that the relationship between the brothers was probably as hostile as the clown, Gordo, had said it was. The charitable view was that Alexei might be taking on the task of calming the situation and trying to keep the circus's routine on foot, but from the conversation with Gordo, he didn't sound the obvious man for the job.

The sound of raised voices heralded the arrival of Izabella, accompanied by some of the other circus people. De Silva recognised the fire-eater and Gordo, but he noted that still no one came forward to introduce himself as Alexei.

Izabella had removed her circus costume and wore a severe, gunmetal-grey dress that clung to her angular figure. No longer warmed by greasepaint, her sallow face looked drained. She stalked over to where Boris and de Silva waited and stopped, regarding him suspiciously. He wondered if gossip and accusations were already circulating backstage. If word had got out that there might have been something wrong with the wire, he was probably not the only one to make the connection to Izabella. Still, if that was the case, the damage was done.

'Miss Rabach, I understand that you and Tatiana checked your equipment before the performance.'

Izabella looked at him blankly and Boris intervened. 'Yes,' she said when he had finished speaking. 'Always I check.' There was aggression in her voice. De Silva saw he would have to handle her with tact, but it was clear she was already on the defensive. He sensed that the mood of the crowd of onlookers, swelled by the arrival of more of the dancers, verged on hostility too. It might be safest to remove Izabella before there was any unpleasantness.

'Everything was good,' she added flatly.

'What time was this?'

She looked at Boris, who said a few words, before she replied.

'Twelve o'clock.'

'Did you check the whole length of the wire?'

Again, she looked to Boris for help then shook her head and said something to him.

'She says no, Tatiana always does this. She only checks where wire is fastened to towers.'

'Did they do the checks together?'

Again a pause while Boris translated.

'No,' he said. 'She does not know when Tatiana checked.'

A man called out from the crowd.

De Silva frowned and turned to Boris. 'What did he say?'

'He saw Tatiana up on wire at about eleven o'clock.'

So, thought de Silva, *Izabella would have had a chance to tamper with the wire after Tatiana's inspection. She might be lying about only involving herself with the fastenings to the towers.* 'When the checks were being done, would there have been lights on as there are now and other people about?' he asked.

'A few,' said Boris. 'But it is high up. People below are busy with their work.' The troubled look on his face had intensified.

'Miss Rabach,' said de Silva. 'While you were up checking the fastenings to the towers as you say you were, did you put anything on the wire? Grease, for example?'

Boris spoke to her again, and she shook her head violently. More people in the crowd shouted out. Concerned by their tone of voice, he made a quick decision.

'I believe it would be best to continue this conversation at the police station. To be clear, at this stage I am not making an arrest.'

Izabella's face darkened as Boris Goncharov translated. She rushed at him, grabbed him by his shirt collar, and began to shake him. A stream of furious words poured from her lips as he forced her back to arm's length and tried to calm her.

De Silva approached the crowd. 'Go about your business. The lady is distressed. Your boss and I will deal with it.'

Mutinous eyes watched him; no one moved.

'Either you leave, or I'll arrest you all for disorderly conduct.' He delivered the order in his sharpest tone, with no idea how many of them understood a word of what he was saying, but he saw Gordo whisper something to his neighbour, who passed it on. Slowly, the crowd backed off. He watched sternly until the stragglers had gone then turned his attention back to Boris and Izabella. He had succeeded in calming her a little although she still shot de Silva looks that would have frozen monsoon rain.

'Izabella will come with you now, Inspector,' said Boris sadly. 'I tell her if she has done nothing wrong, she has nothing to be afraid.'

'I suggest she brings a few things with her. She may be gone for a few days. It's for her safety.'

Boris murmured something to Izabella who wiped her wet cheeks with his handkerchief and nodded.

'I go with her to find Nadia,' he said. 'She will help.'

De Silva omitted to ask who Nadia was; he was already

31

busy thinking about how he would get Izabella to the police station. If she lost her temper again, he didn't relish the idea of sharing the Morris with a wildcat. Fortunately, he heard familiar voices, and Prasanna and Nadar came into the tent. He went over to them.

'You've turned up at the right time. Who told you I was here?'

'Doctor Hebden, sir,' replied Prasanna. 'We asked him if you wanted help. He said he wasn't sure, but he expected you'd be glad of the offer. We're sorry not to have come sooner. We needed to find neighbours who would take our families home.'

'That's fine. You see this lady?'

Prasanna and Nadar peered nervously at Izabella who favoured them with a malevolent stare.

'She's not under arrest, but I need her taken down to the police station. She is to stay there overnight, to keep her safe. I'll come and see her in the morning. If she does try to leave, however, you will have to arrest her. At the moment, she's the most likely suspect we have.' It was, after all, a strong possibility that out of jealousy, Izabella had played a malicious prank on Tatiana that had gone horribly wrong.

'Where must she sleep, sir?' asked Prasanna.

'It will have to be in one of the cells. Make her as comfortable as possible. Plenty of blankets, and all the pillows you can muster. Offer her tea.'

A look of comical dismay came over Prasanna's and Nadar's faces.

'I'm relying on you,' said de Silva briskly.

He had thought of telling Prasanna to come back once Izabella was installed at the station, but on reflection, he would let him stay with Nadar to watch her. Safety in numbers. Presumably, it was too late to catch Hebden, and the cars from the Residence would be long gone. The three of them, and whatever luggage Izabella wanted to bring with her, would have to travel by rickshaw. He sent Prasanna and Nadar off to find a couple of drivers and tell them to wait nearby.

*　*　*

Izabella returned with Boris and a short, plump woman dressed in black. She carried a small holdall and had a grey coat draped over one arm. Talking quietly to Izabella, she steered her in de Silva's direction; he assumed she was the Nadia that Boris had referred to. At close quarters, he saw she was middle-aged with a weathered face netted with wrinkles. She wore a scarf that covered her hair except for a few wiry, grey strands that escaped around her forehead. Her hands were roughened: the hands of a woman who had worked hard all her life. Amber eyes took him in at a glance. He had the feeling that crossing her would be perilous.

'Izabella is ready,' she said. She had the same accent as Boris and Gordo, so presumably, she too was Russian but spoke some English.

Prasanna and Nadar returned with the news that two rickshaws had been found and were waiting outside one of the public exits. With Izabella and her luggage safely installed, de Silva watched the rickshaw men pedal away in the direction of town. When they had dwindled to specks in the gathering darkness, his thoughts went back to Alexei. Where was the fellow?

Inside the tent, he found Boris alone. The ringmaster looked exhausted. 'Nadia sits with Tatiana,' he said. 'She will stay with her tonight. It is hard for her. She has looked after Tatiana since she was baby.'

'What is her role in the circus?' asked de Silva.

'She is wardrobe mistress.'

There was a pause. 'The doctor is arranging for the undertakers to come up to collect Tatiana's body,' continued

33

de Silva. 'But I don't expect it will be before morning now.'

Boris frowned, and it crossed de Silva's mind that he was going to object. It was a delicate situation. As Archie had said, these people were not British; they might not see themselves as obliged to abide by British authority. If Boris refused to give up Tatiana's body, what should he do? He put the question aside, hoping it might not arise.

'Izabella will give your men no trouble,' Boris said at last. 'She gave her word.' His voice cracked and a few moments passed before he composed himself again. 'You think she did this?' he asked wretchedly.

'I'm not sure yet.'

'Do you have more questions?'

'Only one more thing for the moment. As your brother is part owner of the circus, it would be appropriate for me at least to meet him before I leave.'

Boris shrugged. 'If you want. I expect he is found now.'

But if so, why hadn't Alexei made himself known? De Silva was casting about for a way of posing the question that was not too blunt when he heard Boris grunt something.

'I'm sorry, what did you say?'

'I know what you think, Inspector.' With a bitter laugh and a shake of the head, Boris gave de Silva a sideways glance. 'Alexei does as he wants. I am sorry, but I have no power over him. We see if he is found, but if he does not like to speak with you …'

De Silva frowned. The circumstances were out of the ordinary, and Alexei, like Boris, was likely to grieve deeply for someone he had regarded as a sister, but he was a grown man. Tact and sympathy were one thing, pure indulgence another. If necessary, Alexei might have to be compelled to speak with him.

* * *

By the time they emerged from the tent, the last rays of the sun burnished the sky; the green vistas of tea terraces had turned to grey. All the visitors from town had departed. Soon, dusk would give way to night.

A passing circus hand told them which direction the search party had last been seen going in so they followed, heading away from the centre of the course, aiming for the crossing over the track itself and the area where the paddock and the permanent buildings were situated. Darkness gathered as they walked. Stumbling on a tussock of sandy grass, de Silva wished he had brought the torch that he kept in the Morris.

Boris appeared to be untroubled by the rough going, seemingly lost in a world of his own. With his long legs he walked fast, and when they reached the area where the small accommodation tents were pitched, de Silva allowed himself to fall behind, observing the groups of people huddled around the fires outside. They would be glad of the warmth later, he thought. Heat escaped rapidly into a clear night sky, and the racecourse was higher than the town. In a few hours, it would be much cooler, and by dawn, a chill would be nipping fingers and noses.

Aromas of strong, sweet tea and tobacco drifted towards him. Outside a larger tent than the rest, metal grids were heated over big pans of glowing charcoal. Cooks called orders to underlings carrying out platters of raw meat and vegetables. There was a smell of baking bread. It reminded de Silva that he had gone without those tasty snacks he had hoped for, and lunch had been many hours ago.

Despite the semblance of domesticity, however, de Silva sensed an uneasy atmosphere – a mood that made him doubly thankful that by now, Izabella was probably safe at the police station. Firelight washed faces with crimson and gave dark eyes a sinister gleam; muffled conversation, but little laughter, reached his ears. An eerie feeling that he was a spy walking through an enemy camp on the eve of battle crept up on de Silva.

He reproached himself for being so fanciful. These people were bound to be unsettled. Once more, his disapproval focused on Alexei. He could have been out here talking to the groups. The sudden and tragic death of a colleague would alarm and distress most people, quite apart from a fear of it bringing bad luck.

Boris was by now a considerable way ahead, so he quickened his pace to catch up. But before he reached him, Boris suddenly lumbered into an ungainly trot. Several men were hurrying towards them from an area to the right of the racecourse buildings. They were shouting. Boris speeded up, stumbled, and almost fell, but managed to right himself and plough on. De Silva's heart thudded against his ribcage as he began to run too, straining but failing to hear what the men were shouting about; they must be speaking in Russian.

At last, they and Boris met. When de Silva joined them a few moments later, he had already sunk to his knees. It was the snake charmer who seemed to have taken command. De Silva remembered that he and Reverend Peters had met to talk about snakes, so unless the vicar spoke Russian, this man must be able to speak at least some English or one of the local languages. He tried English and asked what had happened.

'We find Alexei,' the man said. 'Please come.'

CHAPTER 3

They took the dirt track on the right going in the direction that the snake charmer and the other men had come from. As they went, de Silva quickly ascertained that the snake charmer's name was Kumar, and he spoke Tamil as well as English. To their left, the racecourse stands and the permanent buildings where the bookies' counters, bars, and other refreshment places were situated were in darkness, although a few lights shone in the area for which they were aiming.

The place they arrived at was a courtyard with buildings on three sides. The doors of the large wooden barn on the left were wide and high; oil lanterns hung on either side of them and on the walls in several other places in the courtyard. To his right, de Silva saw a long, low brick building; a sign to one side of the door indicated it was an office. The building ahead of him was more of a shed, open at the front and with several bays. It seemed to be a storage place for the machinery and equipment needed for maintenance of the racecourse. There were numerous large mowing machines and grass rollers, stacks of posts and rails for fencing, piles of sacks, bales of straw, wheelbarrows, and also, a large muck heap. The smell of fresh horse dung mingled with the musty aroma of chaff in the air.

The rest of the men in the search party hung back, and Kumar took charge. 'This way,' he said, pausing to unhook an oil lantern from a wall before heading for the office building. The door was open, and they went inside.

It had been too wet for race meetings over the monsoon season that had recently come to an end, and apparently the building had not been used for some time. The windowpanes were coated with a thin layer of mouse-grey dust that let in only a little light. De Silva saw serviceable desks and along the wall opposite the door, a row of metal filing cabinets. Above them, noticeboards covered with green baize and lattices of rubber webbing bristled with hundreds of pieces of dog-eared paper: presumably office memos and messages. Instead of horse dung and chaff, he smelled stale tobacco.

At the far end of the room, the word "Manager" was painted on a door that was ajar. As he and Boris followed Kumar and his lantern through the gloom, de Silva felt as if he were swimming through murky water in pursuit of coral fish.

All at once, Boris stopped abruptly. For a moment he froze before barging past Kumar, almost knocking the oil lantern out of his hand in his haste to get into the room. De Silva hung back, a premonition of what he was about to see chilling his blood. A visceral cry reverberated down the length of the building then Boris emerged from the room, his knuckles pale against the dark-stained wood as he clutched the door jamb. 'How this happen?' he asked brokenly. 'Why no one stop him?'

* * *

Limp as one of the sacks in the shed outside, Alexei's body hung from a ceiling beam. A chair lay on its back a little way off. Boris put his arms around his brother and clasped him as if he would never let go. 'Alexei, Alexei,' he mumbled.

'We ought to cut him down,' muttered Kumar. He produced a knife from his belt and went over to Boris, speaking quietly to him until he released his brother's body and went to slump in the chair behind the manager's desk.

The thick rope took several minutes to cut; de Silva supported Alexei's body as Kumar did so. After they had laid Alexei's body on the floor and removed the noose, de Silva glanced at Boris. His expression was blank, and his eyes glazed; he was in no condition to take charge.

'I don't want to leave Alexei here,' said Kumar in Tamil. 'Maybe we should take him to the place where Tatiana's body has been put.'

He said something to Boris in Russian. De Silva couldn't understand it, but presumably Boris agreed with the plan, for Kumar went outside and came back with two fence posts and a bundle of sacks. Working with his knife and some twine, he constructed a makeshift stretcher.

'Will you help me, Inspector?'

De Silva nodded and together they rolled Alexei's body onto it. As they lifted the stretcher, de Silva saw the weave of the material distort, and he feared it might give way, but it held.

It helped that although Alexei was not much shorter than his brother, he was thin as a whip. Dark hair that fell in glossy waves to his shoulders and handsome, chiselled features gave him a romantic air. His smooth skin was tanned; the red wheals and bruising at his neck looked raw and grotesque against the white of his open-necked shirt.

Slowly, with Boris following, they edged the stretcher out of the office building into the yard. The men in the search party were still there, talking quietly and looking as if they were waiting to be told what to do.

De Silva glanced at them. 'I don't want this news getting out yet,' he murmured to Kumar. 'Tell them they are to say nothing until they're told otherwise.'

'Very well.' Kumar spoke briefly to the men who nodded, then one of them took de Silva's end of the stretcher and they set off across the yard. They passed the return journey to the circus in silence, succeeding in skirting the tented camp where fortunately, most people were now occupied with their evening meal.

'That was Alexei's tent,' said Kumar quietly as they passed one. 'But we go this way.'

In the tented room where Tatiana's body lay under a sheet, they set the stretcher down. Apart from the body, the tent was deserted. Nadia must have had to go on some errand for a while.

'I'll find her,' said Kumar. 'She needs to be told.'

De Silva looked in Boris's direction. Once again, he seemed to be in a world apart. He would need to rouse himself soon. The rest of the circus people had to know what had happened, and it would be best if they found out in an official announcement from Boris. But bad news had a way of getting out when one didn't want it to. Despite their nods to Kumar, de Silva wasn't sure that the men in the search party, who were already melting away, were entirely to be relied upon.

'Will you stay with him?' asked Kumar.

'Of course.'

As he went away, de Silva reflected that if his behaviour was anything to go by, the snake charmer must be a more active participant in the affairs of the circus than he had realised. It was just as well; from the look of Boris Goncharov, he was going to need help for quite some time. It seemed that this woman, Nadia, was important too. He remembered Boris saying that she'd looked after Tatiana since she was a baby. She may have been close to the Goncharov brothers as well.

It was clear that Boris did not want to talk, so while he waited for Kumar to come back, de Silva left him in peace and went outside through the exit from the short corridor. The camp was in view, and voices and clattering from the cooking area drifted towards him. Where fires were still burning, bursts of sparks flared, but already some people had damped them down and gone inside their tents. Yes, it was far better that they had a quiet evening and hopefully a good night's sleep before hearing the news of the second tragedy.

Nadia appeared followed by Kumar. In the room where the bodies lay, she went over to Boris and, putting her arms around him, began to croon something that sounded to de Silva like words of comfort. When she looked up, she spoke to Kumar in Russian.

He went over to a trunk in one corner and came back with a long black cape lined with red silk. 'Alexei used it sometimes in his act,' he said, draping it carefully over the body. 'I'll go and tell the other riders to bring the horses in,' he added when the cape was arranged to his satisfaction. 'Usually, I help Alexei with that, and it should have been done already. We let them out to graze in the day on some land we are permitted to use, but at night they must be in the barn in case wild animals are about. If the other riders ask why Alexei is not here, what shall I tell them?'

'For tonight, just tell them that Alexei is unwell. I'll wait for you here.'

Kumar thanked him and departed on his errand. Nadia followed, taking Boris with her.

Left alone, de Silva went to sit on a bench. For a while, he contemplated the two shrouded bodies. There were questions to which he wanted answers. When they came back, maybe Kumar and Nadia would be the people to provide them. He wondered about Kumar's relationship with the dead man. Considering Alexei had other riders working with him, Kumar seemed to be taking on a responsibility for the horses that one would not ordinarily expect. The first thing he wanted to find out, however, was the nature of the connection between Tatiana and Alexei. Was there more to it than the fact of having grown up together? He still suspected that Tatiana's death had not been an accident, and it was so close to Alexei's. His death also raised more questions about Izabella's case. Were the three linked, and if so, how?

He was still deep in thought when Nadia returned.

'I give medicine to help him sleep,' she said.

She went to the table where Alexei lay under the cape and folded it back a little way to expose his face. De Silva saw her fingers tremble as she gently touched the swollen, discoloured flesh at his throat. 'My Alexei,' she said softly. 'My beautiful boy. How can you do this?'

She fell silent, and de Silva waited for her to go on. When she did not, he prompted her as gently as he could. He wanted to find out more about the Goncharovs. It was always useful to know who you were dealing with. But in the circumstances, it was probably best to let her take her time.

Nadia's English was not as good as Boris's or Gordo's. Frequently, she broke off from what she was saying to stroke Alexei's hair and weep, but slowly de Silva learnt that she came from a poor family of ten children. Her parents had been the tenants of a small farm, but it had not produced enough to feed the whole family. When she was twelve years old, she had been taken in by the Goncharovs as a kitchen maid. The work sounded hard, but the family were kind to her. Eventually, she had been allowed to leave the kitchens and help in the nursery. Boris and Alexei were only a few years old, and the family also had a daughter, but she died when she was a baby. Nadia thought that was why the Goncharovs had been happy to take Tatiana in when she was orphaned.

Probing further, de Silva learnt that Tatiana's parents

had been killed by the communists, and not long after they had rescued her, the Goncharovs decided to leave Russia. They had managed to get papers appointing themselves guardians for Tatiana to avoid any difficulties that might arise when they took her with them. Since leaving Russia, they had led a roaming life with the circus.

It must have been a big adjustment to make, thought de Silva. He wondered whether the family business had been a circus before that. And if it had, had it been a successful one?

When he asked about the business, Nadia explained that the boys' father, Ivan Goncharov, had been a very successful man. His own father had built up a well-regarded touring circus, but Ivan was not content to stop there. By the time he had finished, he owned several theatres in St Petersburg and Moscow as well as two more circuses. The family spent the winters in St Petersburg and the summers in the country.

So, the Goncharov brothers had been born to wealth, thought de Silva.

'Was the relationship between the brothers good?' he asked.

'Boris Ivanovich was hero for little Alexei. He climb the tall tree, catch the big fish, swim like eel. But Alexei Ivanovich best with horses. He speak to them; they understand.'

She replaced the cape over Alexei's face and bowed her head for a few moments. De Silva saw her lips move and waited. She might be praying.

'From day Tatiana Petrovna talk,' she resumed at last, 'she follow brothers like little dog. Boris Ivanovich very patient with her. Alexei not so much. I try teach him, but,' she crossed herself, 'sometimes there is devil in him. One moment kind, the next angry—' She spread her hands in a despairing gesture. 'There is no talking with him. Now is different between him and Boris Ivanovich too. Alexei Ivanovich handsome. All girls fall in love with him. At first, Boris Ivanovich laugh, but when Alexei take girls he like, he does not laugh. Then Tatiana Petrovna grow up. She and Alexei—'

Leaving Alexei's body, she went to where Tatiana lay and turned the sheet back from her face. The lovely features that had been so mobile and alive were now set into the waxen mask of death, the sparkling eyes closed for ever. 'I tell you,' she muttered, a fierce edge suddenly sharpening her voice. 'I tell you. Alexei, Boris? Boris, Alexei? No play with fire.'

De Silva frowned, trying to piece together the implications of her remarks. Had both the brothers been in love with Tatiana? Had she played them off against each other, or had she favoured Alexei as other girls had done? Nadia had said Alexei had a volatile temperament. Was it possible that, after a quarrel, he'd had something to do with Tatiana's accident and then killed himself? Or was Boris the guilty party? His sorrow appeared to be genuine, but he wouldn't be the first murderer to know how to dissemble, or indeed to regret his actions when it was too late. And if either of those scenarios was the correct one, where did it leave Izabella? Might she be an accomplice?

'Do you mean that Alexei and Tatiana were lovers?' he asked Nadia.

She nodded. 'Yes. But often, not happy. All the time, they quarrel. This is what happen,' she added bitterly.

'As far as you know, did Alexei have any other troubles that might have led him to kill himself?'

Nadia turned away and he waited for her to answer in her own time. At last she shook her head. 'No.'

'When the high wire was taken down after the accident, it seemed to have been tampered with.'

'Tampered?' she asked hesitantly.

De Silva rephrased the sentence. 'Made slippery with grease.' He mimed a sliding motion with his hands. 'We think that may have been why Tatiana fell.'

Nadia nodded. 'This is why you take Izabella.'

'Yes, but it is partly for her own protection. She may be innocent.'

Looking wary, Nadia waited for him to go on.

'Do you think she would be capable of such an act?' he asked.

She frowned, deepening the wrinkles. 'She jealous of Tatiana. People will say she do this.'

'But do you believe it?'

'Maybe,' she said quietly, after a long pause.

'Thank you. Now, I'd like you to tell me more about Tatiana and Alexei,' he continued. 'You say they quarrelled often. Did Alexei ever tell you he wanted to hurt Tatiana?'

Nadia hid her face, her shoulders heaved, and her muffled words were indistinguishable. When she raised her head, wiping tears from her cheeks, her eyes were red-rimmed.

'Alexei love her. If he do such terrible thing, is because he go crazy.'

De Silva saw the misery in her face. He was sure she had already considered the possibility that Alexei had a hand in the accident. She began to cry again, and it took her a few moments to regain her composure.

'What about Boris?' asked de Silva when she had done so. 'Did he ever threaten either of them?'

Nadia's eyes widened in horror. 'Never! Boris Ivanovich is good man.'

She looked as if she might weep once more so, quickly, de Silva asked if she knew what would happen to Alexei's share of the circus. Apparently their father, Ivan, had anticipated a situation where one brother might die or wish to give up the business. In that event, he had made them promise that the other one would have the sole right to continue the business but must also provide for any widow or children his brother left behind him. Tatiana had the right to work for the circus for as long as she wanted but could never become an owner.

Now that he had an answer to the important question of who stood to benefit from Alexei's death, de Silva only half listened as Nadia drifted into long, sorrowful reminiscences of the Goncharovs' childhood. It might have been idyllic, but the grown-up relationship between the brothers had clearly been difficult. Add into the mixture their seeming rivalry over Tatiana, along with the arrangements for the circus imposed by their father, and the possibilities for conflict and dangerous emotions were enormous. There was no getting away from the fact that, whatever Nadia said, Boris had to be regarded as a suspect.

He thought of Izabella and wondered whether he ought to rule her out of the picture, but then decided it was too soon for that. He hoped that Prasanna and Nadar had managed to placate her. It was hard to know whether she would be more ferocious if she was released than she had been when she was detained. He was quite sure, however, that at the very least there would be glares that could turn water to ice.

* * *

Leaving Nadia to her sad vigil, de Silva walked through the camp once more. Now, all the small fires outside the tents were damped down for the night, and the circus folk had gone to bed. He heard the low murmur of voices, and the grunts and snores of sleepers, but no one accosted him. He was relieved not to have to face any questions.

When he reached the racecourse buildings, he bore right along the track they had taken earlier that evening.

He hoped he might find Kumar with the horses. It would be useful to find out if he backed up Nadia's story.

In the courtyard one of the big doors to the barn was open, so he looked in. The interior was dimly lit, with only a couple of oil lanterns burning. Horses drowsed or ambled about, some pulling at nets of hay, some drinking from the large metal water trough fixed to one wall of the barn. There was a bench close by and de Silva noticed that a wicker basket sat underneath. Its lid was hinged in the centre so that either side could be lifted up independently. It reminded him of the one Jane used for their picnics.

Kumar was brushing a grey mare that was hitched by a halter to a post. When the mare noticed de Silva's arrival, she fidgeted and tossed her head. Kumar made a soothing sound as he steadied her. 'Are you looking for me, Inspector?' he asked in Tamil when she was under control.

'Yes; your boss is asleep, and I've been talking with Nadia, but there are a few things that I hope you'll help me with.'

'Of course, but if it is about the Goncharovs, Nadia knows more than I do.' He shook his head and sighed. 'This will be a big sadness for her.'

'She told me something about the relationship between the brothers, but I'd be interested to hear your opinion.'

Kumar frowned. 'They often fought, but I think there was also respect. Alexei knew his brother was better at running the circus. But Boris knew his brother was good in another way.'

'Do you mean with the horses?'

'Yes. The show was—' Kumar seemed to be searching for the right adjective. 'The best I have seen, and I have seen many.'

'What can you tell me about his relationship with Tatiana?'

'They were lovers, but if Alexei had asked me, I would

have told him to keep away.' He turned his attention back to brushing the mare. 'But I will not speak badly of the dead.'

De Silva felt a stab of impatience. 'If it is something important, you must tell me,' he said sternly.

Kumar frowned. 'Many people liked Tatiana, but she was selfish as well as beautiful. She did not make Alexei happy. I think she liked to make him jealous.'

'Was that with any other man in particular? Boris for example?'

'I think Boris was in love with her once, but he was wise and got over it.'

'But Nadia mentioned he was not happy about the affair. Did you ever hear him threaten to harm either of them?'

'No. If he wasn't happy, it was because their quarrels made trouble in the circus.'

'If she didn't make Alexei jealous over Boris, who else was there?'

Kumar shrugged. After more pressure, de Silva managed to prise it out of him that Tatiana had been in the habit of attracting admirers when the circus stayed in the larger places that they visited for longer than they planned to do in Nuala. She had never bothered to hide her escapades. 'I think Nadia did not tell you that,' Kumar finished.

She certainly hadn't; her account of Tatiana had glossed over this less pleasant aspect of her character.

Kumar finished brushing the grey mare, slipped off the halter and stroked her ears. 'All done, Anoushka. Here, I have a reward for you.' He took something out of his pocket and cupped it in his palm. The mare whickered, delicately drew back her lips and took it. De Silva smelled peppermint.

'Her favourite,' said Kumar with a smile. He gave her a slap on the rump, and she ambled away.

'Once, Tatiana tried it with me,' Kumar went on. He grinned. 'I admit I was tempted, but I decided it wasn't worth the risk of waking up in the night with Alexei's knife at my throat. He was dangerous when he was angry. And he could be angry over very small things.'

'Is there anything else you can tell me about Alexei?'

Kumar thought for a few moments then shook his head.

'Do you know if he had tried to kill himself before?'

'No, but when they argued, he said that sometimes he told Tatiana he would kill himself. She only laughed.'

'Did you often help Alexei with the horses?'

'When I had time. My father was a blacksmith. As a boy, I was often with horses.'

'Were you with the circus in Russia?'

'I've never been there. I joined in India. My family is from Madras.'

He went over to the water trough and checked the level of water. Reaching for a broom that leant against the wall nearby, he started to sweep some wisps of straw into a corner. 'Is there anything else you want to know?'

'Izabella Rabach... what's your opinion of her?'

Kumar grinned. 'As sour as an unripe mango, but I doubt she had anything to do with this. She never spoke more than a few words to Alexei.'

'I have evidence that points to the high wire having been tampered with to cause Tatiana's accident.'

Kumar's eyebrows went up. 'You think Izabella is responsible?'

'It's something we have to consider.'

'She was no friend of Tatiana's, but she has a good living here. I don't think she would risk losing it out of spite.'

Perhaps he was right, thought de Silva, but if that pointed to Alexei being the one who greased the wire, when would he have done it? Presumably after Tatiana checked, but would it have been before or after Izabella did? If the former, he had taken the risk of her noticing something was wrong, so it was more likely to have been after. That wouldn't have given him a great deal of time before the tent became busy with final preparations for the show. And if his death had been suicide, when did that happen? De Silva began to regret that he had not called Hebden back when the body was found. It would have been useful to have his view on the time of death. By the time he saw the body now, it might be too late for him to form an opinion.

'Do you know where Alexei was this morning?' he asked Kumar.

'I was with him when I helped him turn the horses out to graze. That was about eight o'clock. After that, I left him to see to the two that were lame. I had my own work to do.'

De Silva shuddered inwardly at the thought of Kumar's work.

'So it was true that there were lame horses then?' he asked.

'Yes, did someone say it wasn't?'

'No, I just wanted to be sure. Thank you for your help.'

CHAPTER 4

Returning home, de Silva was about to open the front door when he felt a gentle pressure against his right leg. He bent down and picked up the black kitten. 'Good evening, Bella.'

Her jade eyes, splintered with dark pupils, regarded him solemnly then she purred and nuzzled his shoulder.

'I'm not at all sure you should be out at this time of night. What if we lost you?'

In the space of a few months Bella, who had attached herself to him in particular, had wrapped herself around his heart in a way that he had not expected when he had agreed to let her and her brother, Billy, come to live at Sunnybank. Jane was usually meticulous about shutting both of them in at night when wild animals might be prowling the garden, so if Bella was out, the verandah doors must be open and Jane still up.

As he walked down the side path that led to the back garden, he smelled the heady perfume of the ginger lilies in the bed that ran along the house wall. Their white, butterfly-shaped flowers glowed in the shadows. He bent to avoid a low branch of bougainvillea, shifting Bella to his other arm, but she jumped down and ran ahead of him.

Jane looked up from her book. Billy snoozed under the small table beside her chair. 'Hello, dear,' she said with a smile.

'Had you given me up?' He yawned, weary now that the first stage of the investigation was over.

'You look worn out. Have you eaten?'

He shook his head. 'For once, I'm past wanting to.'

'I'll make sure you have extra breakfast.'

'That will do me nicely.'

'If you're too tired to tell me what's been happening, it can keep until morning.'

'No, I think it might clear my head to go over things.'

He explained about the grease on the wire and the suspicion that it had been a malicious trick Izabella had played out of jealousy.

'What did she say when you challenged her?' asked Jane.

'She denied it.'

He went on to tell her about the discovery of Alexei's body, his conversations with Nadia and Kumar, and what Kumar had told him about Tatiana's behaviour.

'How dreadful. It's hard to credit that such a lovely young woman would behave so unkindly.'

'I'm sure your Shakespeare had something pithy to say about appearances deceiving.'

'I expect he did, but what a terrible price for Tatiana to pay for her thoughtlessness and Alexei for his jealousy.' She looked at him shrewdly. 'That is, if you believe that he planned her death then caused his own. Do you believe it?'

He contemplated the question for a moment. 'I'm not sure. We have two people's testimony as to Tatiana's character. Kumar's was less flattering than Nadia's, but then her relationship with Tatiana was much closer than his and of long standing. It's not surprising she saw her in a more sympathetic light. But I heard her words when she bent over Tatiana's body; they intimated that she had warned Tatiana that her behaviour towards Alexei was dangerous, and there was real feeling in her voice. When I pressed her she agreed, albeit unwillingly, that Izabella might have meddled with the high wire, but I believe she also thinks Alexei was capable of playing a part.'

'Then what makes you doubtful?'

'I gathered from Kumar and Nadia that Alexei was extremely moody and had an explosive temper. Would a man like that hatch a cold-blooded plot to kill his lover? Wouldn't he be far more likely to lash out in the heat of the moment?'

'That's a good point; a premeditated crime does sound out of character. And would he have been able to get up to the wire to tamper with it?'

'He was a slim man, and I expect he was agile enough, but if anyone had seen him, they would have thought it very suspicious he was up there. He would have needed to find a time when there was no one about. Whether that would have been possible is something I still need to find out. I can't yet discount the possibility that it was Izabella. Perhaps he persuaded her to do it for him.'

'Surely, in that case you would need to establish there was something between her and Alexei that made her prepared to help him? Jealousy of Tatiana alone might not be enough, but I suppose she could have been in love with him.'

De Silva mulled the point over. 'I'm not convinced the reaction I saw was that of a woman who had been duped by a lover. There was anger, but not sadness.'

'Then Alexei might have promised her promotion.'

'Boris seems more in control of that side of things. And something else is strange, now I come to think of it.'

'What's that?'

'Since Alexei wasn't performing that afternoon, how would he know that Tatiana had suffered her fatal fall? Did he watched unnoticed in the shadows of the auditorium before returning to the stables and a lonely death?'

'So, if Alexei didn't plan Tatiana's fall and then kill himself, who do you suspect?'

'Kumar told me that Boris had once been in love with

Tatiana. He might have been bitter that she chose Alexei instead of him. I've also discovered what will happen to Alexei's share of the circus.' He explained what Nadia had told him.

'So, he has a financial motive too,' said Jane. 'That *is* interesting.'

'It certainly is.'

In his mind's eye, he saw Boris's big, meaty hands encircling his brother's throat, choking him until he lost consciousness, then dragging his helpless body to that grim little room where the final act of the murder was played out.

'He might have hoped to get away with the killings because people would believe Alexei tampered with the wire then died by his own hand, pursuing some violently jealous plan for him and Tatiana to die together. I can't imagine Boris climbing up to that high wire, but he, rather than Alexei, might have been the one who persuaded Izabella to help him in return for promotion to Tatiana's starring role. He hasn't pursued the line that it must have been Izabella who tampered with the wire, but is that because he's a fair-minded man, or is there a more sinister reason? I regret not calling David Hebden back to look at Alexei's body now,' he went on. 'But I don't like to telephone him so late, so it will have to wait until morning. He's off on a fishing trip with some old friends, but I'm sure he'd postpone his departure for an hour or so.'

'If the suicide was a sham to cover up murder, do you think there would be signs?'

'I don't know, but it's worth asking Hebden.'

'But that still won't tell you for sure whether Izabella was involved.'

'No, but that's another point where Hebden's opinion at the time we found the body might have helped me. If it's likely Alexei was dead before Tatiana made her check at around eleven o'clock, then it's hard to credit he was the one who greased the wire. I'm sure Tatiana would have noticed. But if it was later on, it might have been him, or indeed Izabella.'

'That's true. What will you do with Izabella tomorrow?'

'Hold her for a while longer if possible. I haven't arrested her, but I think she's safer where she is. Boris has yet to tell all the circus people about Alexei's suicide, if that's what it was, and I wouldn't be surprised if there aren't rumours circulating about her involvement in Tatiana's fall. I understand that she hasn't many friends in the circus.'

Billy eased himself out from under Jane's chair and padded off in the direction of the garden, attracted by a small cloud of moths hovering over a patch of canna lilies. Jane stood up to fetch him back. 'It's time you were inside,' she said firmly, scooping him under her arm. He emitted a plaintive meow.

'I think it's time we all went in,' said de Silva, linking his hands and stretching his arms above his head.

The clock in the drawing room struck twelve. 'Goodness, we haven't sat up so late for a long time,' said Jane.

De Silva smiled ruefully. 'I hope it doesn't have to become a habit.'

'Don't worry, dear. I'm sure you'll get at the truth soon. Perhaps the case will turn out to be straightforward after all. Late at night, things often have a way of seeming more complicated than they really are.'

'I hope so. Oh, talking of complications, there's something I meant to ask you. The clown, Gordo, called Boris and Alexei by the name Ivanovich, not Goncharov. When I asked him why, he said it was polite for him to do so. I pretended to understand because I didn't want to waste time on the point, but really, I didn't.'

'Ah, it's because they're Russians. The way their names work isn't quite like the British one. They have a first name and a surname as we do, but their middle names are derived from the name of their father. So, Ivanovich means son of Ivan; or if it's a woman, the middle name would be Ivanova, meaning daughter of Ivan. The proper word for these middle names is a patronymic. And as the clown said, it would be very disrespectful to call an adult by their first name alone unless you were a relation or a close friend.'

He grinned. 'I was sure you'd have the answer. I often wonder how you know all these things.'

'I haven't met many Russian people, but I have read a lot of Russian literature,' said Jane with a smile. 'Now, time for bed. And try not to let the case keep you awake. As I said, I expect it will turn out to be much more straightforward than you anticipate.'

'You're probably right.'

But as he locked up, de Silva found it hard to feel reassured. He went into the hall where Billy and Bella were now curled up in their shared basket. Bella raised her head and looked at him, her jade eyes unfathomable.

'What do you think about it, young lady?' he asked.

She meowed then closed her eyes and tucked her head under a front paw.

Sleep: it was sensible advice.

CHAPTER 5

Sleep worked its alchemy, and when he woke the following morning, de Silva was ready to face the day. As he washed and shaved, he made a mental note to telephone the undertaker and warn him that he had two bodies to collect from the circus. He hoped the errand would go smoothly. It occurred to him that the legal position was not clear-cut. The circus people were neither British nor Ceylonese. What if Boris refused to hand over Tatiana's and Alexei's bodies? He hoped common sense would prevail. It also crossed his mind that he would need to be tactful when the question of funeral arrangements came up. The Church of England service that the British were accustomed to might be inappropriate, problematic, or both.

Jane was already at the breakfast table when he came into the dining room. As he sat down and shook his napkin into his lap, she poured him a cup of tea. Stirring in a teaspoon of sugar, he savoured the fragrant scent of bergamot.

'Don't forget you want to telephone David Hebden,' said Jane as he set to work on a hopper filled with two soft-boiled eggs. The bowl-shaped pancake was garnished with sliced onions, fried until the rings were sweet and crispy, and flakes of toasted coconut. There were slices of fresh pineapple and mango to follow, but as he mopped up the last of the egg with a piece of pancake, de Silva decided they would have to wait until he had spoken to Hebden. He didn't want to miss him.

In the hall, he dialled the Hebdens' number and waited. It was answered after several rings by Emerald.

'Forgive me for calling on a Sunday morning,' he said after they had exchanged greetings. 'But I'd like a word with your husband.'

'I'm afraid you've missed him. I've just come in from seeing him off. He and his friends wanted to make the most of the day.'

De Silva grimaced. He should have guessed Hebden would be off early. There was no chance of getting him up to the circus today.

'When do you expect him back?'

'Not until Tuesday, and he might not be here before dinner time. The drive takes several hours, and they want to go fishing in the morning. Is it something to do with the accident at the circus?'

De Silva hesitated. He was sure that Emerald wouldn't gossip if she knew discretion was important, and he didn't want to cause offence by not entrusting her with news of a major development, but neither did he want to spend too much time on the telephone. He explained briefly, adding that Alexei's death was confidential at present; he was glad she didn't ask questions.

'I'm afraid I have no way of contacting David unless he contacts me,' she said. 'I know he'll be sorry not to be able to help straight away.'

'Never mind, my fault for not calling sooner, but I didn't like to disturb you last night. It was late when I came home.'

And this morning, he thought ruefully, *I allowed the dictates of my stomach to take first place.*

'I've just had a thought. You might ask Doctor Norton down at Hatton. He and David have an arrangement to cover each other's cases if one of them is away.'

De Silva considered the idea for a moment. He had come across Norton a few times and he seemed a capable man, but on reflection, as neither doctor would be able to throw much light on the time of death now, it might also be a forlorn hope that they would be able to tell whether Alexei had died from hanging or some other cause. He might as well wait for Hebden's return.

'I don't think a few days' delay will be a serious problem. I won't disturb him on a Sunday.'

'Very well. Shall I ask David to call you when he gets home?'

'I'll drop a note in to the surgery.'

'Well, I'll tell him you rang anyway.'

'Thank you.'

'He'd already left,' he said to Jane when he came back to the dining room. He sat down and pulled the bowl of fruit towards him. 'I shall console myself with some of this.' He sniffed the tangy smell of pineapple and the intense sweetness of mango.

'Do you think it will matter?' asked Jane, spreading Cooper's Oxford marmalade on her toast.

'Probably not too much. Emerald suggested I call Doctor Norton up from Hatton, but I doubt that he will be keen to come on a Sunday, and Hebden is back on Tuesday evening. His opinion can wait. I'll drop a note at the surgery, asking him to have a look at the body as soon as it's convenient after he gets back. He would need to do that anyway for the medical reports for the coroner.'

He took a bite of mango and wiped some juice from his chin with his napkin. 'This is delicious.'

'Will you still go up to the circus?'

His mouth full of another piece of mango, he nodded. 'Yes. But I might pay a visit to Archie first. He asked for a report on the case. I think news of a development like this shouldn't wait until Monday.'

'He and Florence usually come to church on a Sunday.'

He finished his fruit. 'Perhaps it will be easier to telephone. I'll call and see if he's available now.'

Waiting while the servant who answered went to find Archie, de Silva wondered what his boss's reaction to the news would be. Certainly, he had been reluctant to get involved in Tatiana's case, but then her death might genuinely have been an accident. At first, there had been no reason to think otherwise. Alexei's death was a different matter.

The servant came back on the line. 'I am sorry, Inspector, no one can find the sahib. We think he has gone out for a walk.'

'When is he expected back?'

'No one is sure.'

In time for church presumably, but then he would be in a hurry. He thanked the servant and decided to go up in person.

Jane was pouring another cup of tea when he returned to the dining room.

'I'll go to the Residence after all. Archie's out for a walk, and they don't know when he'll be back. Hopefully, I can find him, and there'll be time to have a few words before he wants to be on his way to church.'

'Do finish your breakfast before you go, dear.'

'I've had enough.' He kissed her cheek. 'I'm afraid I may not be back in time to give you a lift to church.'

'Don't worry. I'll manage.'

* * *

It had rained in the night, freshening the trees that lined the road to the Residence and making them sparkle in the sun. Here and there, the bright flash of parrots and other birds contrasted with the greenery. A few puddles of water steamed gently at the sides of the road. One hand resting on the wheel, de Silva almost forgot he was in a hurry.

He wondered again what Archie's reaction would be to the news that they had another body on their hands. If he persisted in the view that British involvement should be kept to the minimum, the conversation might not be an easy one. But whatever Archie's opinion, the deaths had occurred on his, de Silva's, patch. It went against the grain to sweep the matter under the carpet.

He turned the Morris into the Residence's drive. At first, the view of the large white house was partially obscured by tall palm trees, then it became clearly visible. When he had parked the Morris, he went up to the front door and knocked. It was worth checking whether Archie had returned before he trudged around the grounds looking for him.

'The sahib is still not back,' the servant who answered the door told him. 'You might find him down at the fishing lake. The dog likes to swim.'

De Silva thanked him and set off.

The lake that Archie had stocked with fish on his arrival in Nuala, so that he could indulge his fondness for fishing, was a good distance from the house. De Silva walked briskly in its direction, not stopping to admire the gardens as he would usually have done.

Cresting the little rise where the lake came into view, he spotted Archie standing on the bank in the shade of an Indian oak tree whose branches spread out over the water. There was no sign of his dog, Darcy. He was probably enjoying a swim as the servant had suggested.

As de Silva approached, Archie saw him and raised a hand in greeting. Darcy was now visible. He was a good swimmer for an old dog, forging through the calm waters of the lake, looking sleek as an otter.

'Good morning!' Archie called out. 'We're just having our constitutional before it's time to leave for church. Since we don't usually see you up here on a Sunday, I presume you've brought me news of this business at the circus.'

'Yes, sir, and I'm afraid it is not good.'

'Hmm.' Archie frowned. 'Before we go into it, you ought to know there's been a burglary at the de Vere plantation over at Hatton.' De Silva recognised the name of one of the wealthy tea growers. 'It seems thieves broke in on Friday night whilst the family were away,' Archie continued. 'But I only heard about it when Mrs Clutterbuck and I returned from the circus show yesterday evening. Inspector Singh at Hatton had left a message with one of my staff. Mrs de Vere is a great friend of Mrs Clutterbuck's, and she rang to commiserate, so we got more information. You'd better have a word with Singh. Find out if there's anything we need to do. I'm not sure if he has any descriptions and whether we ought to be setting up roadblocks.'

Inwardly, de Silva groaned – he didn't need anything else on his plate – but he nodded. 'I'll get onto it as soon as possible.'

'Right. Now, you'd better tell me what's been happening at the circus.'

'We have another body.'

'Whose body?'

'Boris Goncharov's brother. His name was Alexei.'

'I don't recall him being mentioned last night. Was he one of the performers that we saw?'

'No. I first heard about him from one of the clowns rather than his brother. Apparently, Alexei was in charge of the horses and the acts that involved them, but some of them were lame after the journey up to Nuala and he refused to take part. I understand there was an argument between the brothers about whether it was necessary to abandon the entire act. Boris complained that his brother wasn't doing his job properly.'

'So, was this fellow Alexei's death another accident?' De Silva thought that Archie said it in a rather hopeful tone.

'He was found hanging from a beam in the office

building at the racecourse. There was no sign of a struggle.'

Archie frowned. 'The conclusion has to be suicide, wouldn't you agree? Tragic, but as I said last night, de Silva, these people are not our responsibility. I suggest you get onto Hebden, if you haven't already done so – oh no, I was forgetting, he's away on a fishing trip. Well, get him to deal with the medical reports when he comes back, and then you can pass them on to the coroner's office. Once that's done, it should be a straightforward process for the bodies to be released for burial. You'd better make inquiries about what religious observances these people want. When you've done that, get onto Peters and see what he can do to oblige them.'

'With respect, sir, I'm not sure it is straightforward.'

First, he explained about the stormy relationship between Tatiana and Alexei and the grease on the wire.

'Well, if this fellow was eaten up by jealousy and somehow brought about the accident before killing himself, my point is still valid,' interrupted Archie. 'The episode is tragic, but it's an internal matter for the circus and no affair of ours.' He looked intently at de Silva. 'Do you disagree?'

'Not precisely, sir. If I may go on, I'm not convinced we can wrap the matter up so easily.'

Archie sighed. 'Would you like to expand on that?'

'It's a convenient explanation, but to me, it doesn't ring true. Both the snake charmer, Kumar, and the wardrobe mistress, Nadia, who knew Alexei from when he was a child, described him to me as the impulsive, moody one of the brothers. Kumar said he had a fierce temper and was easily provoked. In my experience, men like that don't plan their revenge in advance, they exact it without warning. I also have my doubts that if he wanted her to die with him, he would have committed suicide and left it to chance that Tatiana's fall would cause her death.'

'Hmm. Say you're right, and the situation isn't cut and dried, who else do you suspect?'

'Izabella Rabach, the artiste who participated in Tatiana's act, had reason to be jealous of her. Boris made it clear that Izabella's abilities exceed the work she had been employed to do. She only took the job because she was in urgent need of work when he offered it to her. She's a proud, temperamental woman. I haven't ruled out that she may have been the one to tamper with the wire. I haven't arrested her, but she's been taken down to the station, partly for her own safety, as the general mood at the circus seems to be against her.'

De Silva thought of Prasanna and Nadar, still in charge of her there. He ought not to leave them to cope unaided for too much longer.

'It's a long way from a bit of jealousy between two women to committing murder. You'll need to come up with something more convincing than that.'

A black head emerged out of the water near to where the oak tree's gnarled roots snaked out over the silty shore. Archie stepped back smartly as Darcy hauled himself out and shook, sending a flurry of spray for several feet. 'Sorry, should have warned you,' said Archie as de Silva wiped his trousers.

Archie picked up a stick and threw it. 'That'll keep him busy while he dries off. Now, where were we? Ah yes, the Rabach woman. Is there any more to your theory that she sabotaged the wire?'

'If Alexei was guilty, he might have put her up to it, but I think it's more likely that she would have done it for the brother, Boris; probably in return for a starring role once Tatiana was gone, or at least unable to perform.'

'Why would he want to get rid of this girl, Tatiana?'

De Silva explained about the rivalry between the brothers over her, and the conditions their father had imposed about ownership of the circus.

'So, you're saying this fellow Boris may have set up the

fall and what looked like suicide to get revenge and for financial gain.' Archie looked dubious.

Darcy, now stretched out on the ground with the stick held between his front paws, had worked it to his back teeth where it split with a loud crack.

Archie looked at his watch. 'I must be getting on, or we'll be late for church, and I won't hear the end of it from Mrs Clutterbuck. By all means, investigate your theory, de Silva. But you know as well as I do that it will take more than a hunch to make it watertight. I don't think a bit of stickiness on the high wire will convince a court. If you haven't unearthed something more concrete pretty soon, I'd advise you to let this Rabach woman go and not waste any more time. And don't forget about speaking to Singh. That's important.'

Leaving Archie to get on with his morning, de Silva drove back into town. His boss's attitude rankled somewhat, but to be fair, he was right about the need for solid evidence. What was little more than a hunch would not justify keeping Izabella in custody for long. Given the choice between charging her with Tatiana's murder on insufficient grounds and letting her go, the latter was probably the wisest option.

But maybe there was another way.

As he passed the church, the bells started to peal for morning service. He hoped Jane had managed to arrange a lift.

* * *

Prasanna's and Nadar's bicycles were chained up outside the police station. He felt a pang of guilt for keeping them on duty all night, but there was safety in numbers.

Quietly entering the public room, he found Nadar dozing on a makeshift bed improvised from two chairs facing each other, a rolled-up blanket under his head, and a thinner one over him. When de Silva cleared his throat, he woke with a start and tumbled to the floor then swiftly picked himself up.

'Sorry, sir,' he gabbled. 'It took a long time to go to sleep last night.'

'At ease, Constable. Where's Prasanna?'

'He was here a little while ago, sir.'

At that moment, Prasanna appeared in the doorway that led to the scullery and the yard at the back of the station. He had a cup of tea in his hand.

'Ah, just in time,' said de Silva. He took in Prasanna's bleary-eyed expression and rumpled hair and grinned. 'I think your need is greater than mine. You can fetch me one when you've finished that.'

'Thank you, sir.'

'How is our guest?'

'Asleep, sir.' Prasanna said the word as warily as if he was talking about a dragon who had temporarily lost interest in breathing fire and decided to take a nap.

'Did she give you any trouble last night?'

'I'm afraid so, sir. We found all the blankets we could and offered her tea as you suggested, but she was not pacified.'

So much for Boris's assurances she would give no trouble.

'I suppose I'd better have a word with her when she's awake. Anything else to report?'

'Inspector Singh telephoned. He asked if you would call him back.'

That must be about the burglary at the de Vere plantation. He gave Prasanna and Nadar what information he had. He realised it was also time that he brought them up to date on events at the circus, so he explained his reservations about Alexei's apparent suicide and the possibility that Izabella was implicated in a plot with Boris.

'Is that why you don't want to release her yet, sir?' asked Prasanna.

'Yes, although even if she's innocent, I think she may need to be shielded from other members of the circus for a while.'

'How will you find out if she is involved, sir?'

'At the moment, I have no idea,' said de Silva ruefully. 'Now, about that tea... And Nadar, would you call Inspector Singh back for me.'

While he waited for Prasanna to bring the tea to his office, he wrote the note to Hebden asking him to look at Alexei's body on his return. Putting it in an envelope, he left it on his desk. There was no hurry; it could be delivered when he next went that way.

The telephone rang with the call to Hatton and Inspector Singh's deep voice came on the line.

'Archie Clutterbuck told me about the de Vere burglary this morning,' said de Silva. 'Is there anything I can do to help?' He devoutly hoped Singh would say there wasn't.

'It's good of you to offer, but not at the moment. Unfortunately, we have no descriptions of the men involved, but I've set up roadblocks with instructions to stop anyone who looks suspicious. I'll keep you informed. Let's hope they're not coming your way.'

'Thank you. We'll keep an eye out.'

'I understand from Archie Clutterbuck that you have problems of your own.'

'Unfortunately, that's the case.'

De Silva gave a brief résumé of events at the circus then wished him goodbye. Shortly afterwards, Prasanna brought the tea. De Silva drank it then readied himself to talk to Izabella.

The corridor leading to the two cells that the Nuala station contained was quiet and dimly lit by a window high up in the wall. This was matched in the lighting of the two cells. In the one she occupied, Izabella Rabach was awake, sitting on the edge of the bed. A baleful expression came over her face when she saw de Silva.

'You have no right keep me,' she spat. 'You come tell me I leave, yes?'

'Not yet, ma'am, but if I had, I'd advise you to think carefully before doing so.'

Izabella scowled. 'What you mean?'

'I imagine it can't have escaped your notice that there was a great deal of ill-feeling against you last night.'

He was not sure whether the suspicious look Izabella gave him was due to her difficulty in understanding what he said or accepting it. He tried again.

'Miss Rabach, you are safer here with us than you will be if you go back to the circus. People are angry.'

She swallowed hard. He wondered if there was going to be an outburst, but instead she began to cry. 'I do nothing,' she said between sobs. 'Why no one help? Where is Boris Ivanovich?'

De Silva realised that if she was innocent, she would have no idea about what had happened to Alexei. He must observe her reaction carefully when he told her.

'I'm afraid it may be a little while before he comes to see you,' he said. 'There has been another tragedy at the circus.'

The blank look Izabella gave him might have been because she didn't understand, or because she was dissembling; he wasn't sure which.

'Boris's brother, Alexei, has been found dead.'

Her jaw dropped, and she stared at him. 'Dead?' she asked in a whisper. 'How is he dead?'

'We believe he killed himself.'

Izabella crossed herself and began to mutter under her breath. De Silva wondered if the language was her native Hungarian. Shivering, she rocked back and forth, as if unaware of what she was doing. It seemed plausible that

Alexei's death had come as news to her. All the same he was convinced that, at least for the moment, it was best to keep her away from the circus. If both she and Boris Goncharov came out of this with their names cleared, how to deal with the problem of her unpopularity and any lingering suspicion of her would be up to Boris, but for now, de Silva felt some responsibility for her.

'Would you like breakfast?' he asked.

'No hungry.'

'You must try to eat something.'

She shook her head.

Ignoring her refusal, he went a little way down the corridor and called for Prasanna. A few moments later, the sergeant appeared.

'Bring tea and something to eat for this lady.'

Prasanna looked perplexed. 'What food shall I bring, sir?'

De Silva glanced back at Izabella. Head bowed, she still sat on the edge of the bed. He imagined that she would have no interest in choosing what to eat.

'Fruit, bread, cheese – nothing too spicy,' he said.

Prasanna departed and a few minutes later, Nadar appeared with the tea. 'Prasanna has gone to the bazaar for the food, sir,' he said. He gave Izabella a nervous glance, but she ignored him.

'Good.' De Silva indicated the small table in the corner. 'Leave the tray on there. I'll see to the rest.'

When Prasanna had gone, de Silva picked up the teapot and poured tea into the cup. 'We have sugar but no milk, I am afraid.'

Izabella made a face. 'In my country, we no drink tea.'

'This is our excellent Ceylon tea. You must try it,' he said patiently.

She came to the table and sat down. De Silva pushed the sugar bowl over to her, but with a shake of her head she pushed it away. Eventually, despite her protestation, she tried a sip of tea and it seemed to revive her. In halting English, but with a somewhat better command of the language now that she was calmer, she answered his questions about her work in the circus and what she had been doing on the previous day. She continued to insist that the grease on the high wire had nothing to do with her, and she stuck to her story of the time she had made her check.

'What did you do when you had finished?' he asked.

'I eat lunch with others. People see me. You ask. After, I walk until it is time to make ready for show. I do not like to be with other people then. My head—' She paused. 'My head needs quiet.'

'You need to concentrate?'

She nodded.

'How long did you walk for?'

'Half of an hour maybe.'

'Did anyone see you?'

Izabella shrugged.

'Do you know when Tatiana made her own inspection?'

'Please?'

'The high wire. When did Tatiana check it?'

'You hear eleven o'clock. Maybe it was then.'

'Were you and Tatiana friends?'

'Friends?'

'Yes.'

'We work together, but not friends.' For the first time, the woman laughed, although the sound was mirthless. 'Tatiana Petrovna and Alexei Ivanovich were good friends.'

So, thought de Silva, their relationship was no secret.

There were footsteps in the corridor, and Prasanna appeared with the food: naan bread, soft cheese, and a selection of fruit. Izabella's appetite must have returned for she tucked in hungrily.

'I'll leave you now,' said de Silva. 'Are you willing to stay here quietly?'

A mutinous look flashed across Izabella's face again, but then her expression softened. 'You are kind. I do as you ask. But I must see Boris Ivanovich,' she added hastily. 'If he not let me stay, I have to find other work. Promise me you speak with him.'

The anxiety on her face made de Silva feel sorry for her. It was clear that she was not a happy woman, but now that he had spent time in her company, he was less inclined than before to believe that she possessed sufficient malice to set out to injure or kill a rival.

'I promise, and I'll come back to see you soon. Meanwhile, my constable will be here if you need anything.'

In the public room, he asked Nadar to remain on watch.

'I want you to come with me,' he said to Prasanna. 'By the way, do your wives know why you didn't come home last night?'

'I sent a boy with a message, sir,' said Prasanna.

'Good. If you like, we'll stop at your house on the way to the circus and explain that you may be gone for some time. We'll ask Kuveni to pass the message on to your wife, Nadar.'

The young men looked disconsolate, but they thanked him.

CHAPTER 6

'You had best get your notebook out,' said de Silva as he drove away from the station with Prasanna.

'Go ahead, sir,' Prasanna said when he was ready with his book and pencil.

'I want to talk to Boris Goncharov again. What I need you to do, is find out when the rest of the circus people last saw him and his brother, Alexei. Izabella Rabach claimed that after she checked her equipment for the show at twelve o'clock, she went to eat with the rest of the crew then walked around for a while on her own; apparently this is something she does to clear her head before a show. She tells me people saw her at the meal, but I want you to make sure she's telling the truth. And find out if anyone saw her walking around afterward. You may as well ask about Tatiana's movements too, and generally, ask if anyone noticed anything out of the ordinary going on before the show yesterday.'

He glanced at Prasanna after he'd finished writing in his notebook. 'You look doubtful, Sergeant.'

'How shall I talk to them, sir? I think most of them only speak Russian.'

'I'm sure we'll find someone to help you.'

Kumar must have picked up quite a bit of Russian in his travels with the circus, thought de Silva, and from his own point of view, it was easy being able to talk to him in

Tamil. On the other hand, the circus people might be more forthcoming with someone of their own nationality. Gordo the clown came to mind. He had been obliging yesterday, and his English seemed reasonably good.

'You'd better tell him about Alexei's death if the news hasn't already got out,' he said when he had told Prasanna who he had in mind. 'But first,' he went on, 'we need something to eat. It might be some time before there's a chance of lunch.'

The Morris idled along the main thoroughfare that bisected the bazaar until de Silva spotted the stall he wanted. Parking the car, he purchased bowls of vegetable curry and rice for them both and they ate it standing up, then after a short stop at Prasanna's home, they set off on the road that led uphill to the racecourse.

As luck would have it, they found Gordo without any difficulty. Like most of the circus folk, he was dozing in the shade at the tented camp. When de Silva explained what he wanted, the clown readily agreed to help. There was no need to tell him about Alexei's death; Boris had called the crew together earlier that morning and made the announcement.

'I'll leave you to it, then,' said de Silva. 'Come and find me when you've finished. If I'm not up here, Prasanna, I'll be waiting for you down at the car.'

* * *

After she had waved de Silva off, Jane telephoned the Hebdens' house. A servant answered, and she waited while he went to fetch Emerald.

'If you're going to church,' said Jane when her friend came on the line, 'would you mind giving me a lift? Shanti has taken the car, and I'm not expecting him back in time.'

'Of course. Shall I pick you up at half past ten?'

'That would be lovely. Thank you.'

She spoke to the cook, and as she would be eating alone, ordered a light lunch, then spent an hour writing letters. At ten o'clock, she put down her pen and went to get ready for church. She had just put on her hat when Emerald drove in.

'David's taken the Land Rover,' she said as Jane slipped into the Austin 7's passenger seat. 'The roads are likely to be rough where they're going. I'm sorry you missed him this morning. He was very keen to be off early.'

'Never mind. Shanti will talk to him when he gets back.'

'Have there been any developments at the circus? Shanti told me Boris Goncharov's brother had been found dead, but I didn't like to detain him with questions. It was obvious he was busy. But David mentioned they found some grease on the high wire, and there might have been foul play.'

'Yes, and that's why Shanti wanted David to see the body. He was hoping he might be able to tell whether Alexei was dead before the rope was put around his neck.'

Emerald frowned. 'That sounds very mysterious. If it was the case, where would it lead?'

'Do you promise not to breathe a word?'

'Of course.'

'Shanti thinks Boris might be involved, but I'd better not say any more.'

'Goodness. Who else knows?'

'Archie does, because Shanti made a report to him, but apparently he isn't showing much interest in the case. Shanti thinks it's because none of the people involved are British, or even local for that matter.'

They had reached the centre of town, where Emerald had to slow down to negotiate bullock carts and wandering pedestrians as well as other cars. 'That doesn't surprise me,' she remarked. 'The people from the Residence I've spoken to recently say all he can talk about is the war in Europe.'

Jane sighed. 'I suppose it's inevitable he's worried, and I'm sure he's not the only one.'

A few minutes later, they turned into the church drive and found a place to park. Up in the church's low square tower, the bells that had been chiming merrily slowed to a solemn, repeating note. Quickening their step, they went through the lychgate to join the queue of people filing in.

Nice as Reverend Peters was, his sermons were never very inspired, thought Jane, as they reached that stage of the service. She wondered whether he wrote them himself or found them in a book; she guessed the latter. He was probably far happier cultivating his orchids, or as Mrs Peters had now divulged, studying snakes, than thinking up and polishing sermons. After he came to the end, there were a few more prayers and a final hymn before the congregation went out into the sunshine, shaking hands with him on the way.

Emerald went to speak to a friend, and Jane heard a familiar voice hail her.

'Good morning!'

She turned to find a smiling Archie with Florence on his arm.

'It's good afternoon now, dear,' said Florence. 'How are you, Jane? Are you by yourself? Can we offer you a lift home?'

'That's most kind of you, but Emerald Hebden is taking me back. She drove us over here.'

'Ah, of course,' said Archie jovially. 'Hebden's away fishing, lucky fellow. I know the stretch of river he and his friends have chosen. A good spot. They should have excellent sport.'

Emerald returned to join them. 'I was just hearing about the burglary at the de Vere plantation on Friday,' she said when greetings had been exchanged. Jane recognised the name of the family who owned one of the largest tea plantations in the Hatton area. It was odd that Shanti hadn't mentioned it.

Florence's chins wobbled as she shuddered theatrically. 'Poor Margaret de Vere was beside herself when I telephoned to commiserate. All her family diamonds have been taken, and most of the jewellery that Henry's given her over the years that they've been married. She only had one or two pieces with her. They'd gone down to Kandy for a few days leaving the house servants in charge.'

'There's no suggestion that any of them are responsible,' said Archie. 'They've all been with the family for many years. And in any case, it must have been a professional job. Whoever took the jewellery had to be capable of cracking the safe where it was kept.'

'The thieves broke in during the night,' Florence went on. 'It makes one afraid to sleep in one's bed.'

'I don't think you need to be anxious, my dear,' said Archie. 'Security at the Residence has been tightened up since the Tankerton business. It's well guarded. Or you, ladies,' he added in a reassuring tone that was, thought Jane, kindly meant, although she wasn't sure how he could be certain.

George and Charlotte Appleby came over to join the little group.

'We were discussing this dreadful burglary at the de Vere plantation,' said Florence.

Charlotte Appleby put a hand to the pretty necklace at her throat.

'Don't worry, Charlotte,' said her husband. 'We have enough dogs around the place to chase off any number of burglars.' The Applebys were well-known for rescuing strays.

'Do you think they'll be caught, Mr Clutterbuck?' asked Charlotte.

'I spoke to Inspector Singh at Hatton this morning. He's pulling out all the stops but it's early days yet.'

'Will your husband be involved, Mrs de Silva?'

Jane noticed Archie give her a sharp look and interpreted it as a warning not to mention that de Silva was likely to be busy with events at the circus. If he was keen to avoid the subject, she had no intention of rocking the boat. She was also feeling a little piqued that this was the first she'd heard of the burglary, and she didn't want it to show. Surely, if Archie knew about it, Shanti must too. It wasn't like him to keep things from her.

'I've no doubt that he'll be happy to help if Inspector Singh needs another pair of hands,' she said.

Florence tapped Archie on the arm. 'We must be on our way, dear. I hope you haven't forgotten we have guests coming to lunch.'

'No, I haven't forgotten.' Archie's tone hinted that he might have preferred a quiet Sunday afternoon snoozing with the newspaper. He tipped his hat. 'A pleasure to see you, ladies. Appleby.'

As they moved off down the path towards the lychgate, Jane found herself walking with George Appleby while Emerald chatted to his wife.

'Emerald tells me you and your husband have acquired two kittens,' he said. Jane recalled that he was the government veterinary officer for the district.

'Yes, they're dear little things. They just turned up in the garden. We think their mother may have been killed by a wild animal.'

Appleby sighed. 'I fear that's not uncommon. Stray cats and dogs are very much at risk from all kinds of dangers. I'm keen to start a programme of neutering to do something to tackle the problem but regrettably, such matters are not a high priority with our political masters.'

Jane frowned. She hadn't given any thought to the issue of neutering.

'I'd advise it if you don't plan to breed from them,' said Appleby when she asked him. 'For the males, it's a common operation that has the added benefit of dissuading them from wandering. It's less common with females. Although advances in veterinary medicine have made the process far safer than it used to be, the procedure is more invasive. Do you know how old they are?'

'We think they were only a couple of months old when we found them, and they've been with us for about six months now.'

'Then if you want to have it done, it's high time. If you like, I'll give them a general check over too. Just give the surgery a call and the receptionist will make you an appointment.'

Jane thanked him and joined Emerald at the car.

'What a nice man George Appleby is,' she remarked as they drove away. 'He was asking about Billy and Bella and made some helpful suggestions. I must speak to Shanti about them.'

'Yes, George takes animal welfare very seriously.'

'I hope you're not worried about being alone while David's away,' said Jane after a short silence.

'Because of the de Vere burglary, do you mean? Gracious no.' Emerald smiled. 'David's very generous, but my collection of jewellery hardly compares with Mrs de Vere's. Anyway, David left Jasper with me. He'd bark the house down if he thought there were intruders about.'

Another silence fell.

'Is something wrong?' asked Emerald.

Jane frowned. 'I'm rather surprised Shanti didn't mention this burglary to me.'

'I expect there's a simple explanation,' said Emerald soothingly.

'Do you think so?'

Emerald nodded, and Jane felt slightly mollified. 'From the sound of it, my collection can't compete with Mrs de Vere's either. But Florence may have more cause for alarm.

I've seen her wearing some pieces that look valuable. Her diamond necklace, and that gold brooch set with emeralds, amongst other things.'

'But Archie said that the Residence is very secure. To say nothing of Angel.'

Jane chuckled. Florence's feisty little household mop of a dog would be a daunting prospect for any burglar who wanted his ankles to remain unscathed.

'Dear old Darcy would just lick them to death,' Emerald added.

She slowed to go through the gate into the drive at Sunnybank and pulled up in front of the bungalow. There was no sign of the Morris.

'As we're both on our own today,' said Jane, 'would you like to join me for lunch? It will just be a light one.'

'A light lunch is perfect. I forgot to arrange anything with our cook, and it's so dull eating alone.'

Jane opened the car door, and Billy and Bella appeared from behind a bush and trotted over. Emerald bent down to stroke them. 'It must be nice that there's always someone to welcome you when you come home.'

'Yes, it is. I can't imagine how we managed without them.'

* * *

Leaving Prasanna and Gordo, de Silva asked the first person he met for the way to Boris Goncharov's tent. In the heat of the day, it was a reasonable place to start looking for him.

As he walked, he was interested to see that the atmosphere around the camp was a little livelier than it had been the previous night. A juggler was practising his skills, the red, yellow and silver balls catching the light as he tossed them in the air. Elsewhere, a contortionist tied himself in a seemingly impossible series of knots. More people in the groups around the tents were talking. Not for the first time, it struck him how remarkable was the human race's ability to recover from a setback.

Nearing the tent where he had been told he would find Boris, he heard raised voices. One of them belonged to a woman and the other he recognised as Boris's. A few steps from the entrance flap, he hung back, not sure that it was advisable to barge in. It was unfortunate that he was not able to understand what was being said, but he had an idea who the woman might be.

A moment later, confirming his guess, Nadia swept out, the expression on her plump face filled with indignation. She flashed him a dismissive look before stomping off. After a prudent pause, he pushed aside the heavy canvas flap and went into the tent.

Boris, who had been facing in the other direction, swung round barking out a string of angry words in Russian, then he stopped; his face shone with sweat and a vein at his temple pulsed with heated blood.

'Good afternoon, sir. I'm sorry to intrude.'

Boris rallied. 'No need for apology,' he grunted, gesturing towards the table and chairs in one corner of the tent. 'Please, sit.'

De Silva followed him and sat down. Boris leant back in his chair with his arms folded over his burly chest. He made the furniture look as if it had been made for a doll's house.

'So,' he said, frowning. 'You have questions?'

'I understand from Nadia that the relationship between your late brother and Tatiana Petrovna was a troubled one. She believes it was what led your brother to end his life, but if you take a different view, I'd be grateful if you would tell me what that is.'

With a sigh that seemed to come from deep down, Boris shook his head. 'No difference.'

'So, as far as you are aware, Alexei had no other serious problems. Over money, perhaps?'

Boris shook his head.

De Silva hesitated. The next question was bound to be a difficult one. Even if Boris no longer harboured romantic feelings for Tatiana, she had been like a sister to him. De Silva had no siblings, but he could imagine the pain of thinking that one might be responsible for another's death.

'Did he ever say, or imply, that he would hurt Tatiana?'

Boris flushed. 'Alexei had bad temper, but I never hear him say this. If someone touch wire, it is Izabella. Or one of my people make mistake and lie to me,' he added grimly.

De Silva saw the flush deepen. He wondered if that was true but decided not to press the Russian.

'When did you last see your brother?'

'On Friday.' He stopped to think. 'About ten o'clock in evening. I get message Alexei will not do show for yesterday.'

'Why was that?'

'Two horses are lame.'

'Did you accept that was a good enough reason?'

'No! I go to speak with him and say put on show with other horses!'

That bore out what Gordo had said.

'We talk, but he does not change mind.' Sadness clouded Boris's face. 'This is like Alexei. I tell him think about it and I come back in morning.' He sighed. 'But in morning I do not. There is much to do, and I do not want fight. Maybe we are friends; maybe not.'

If Boris was innocent, de Silva felt sorry for him. For the rest of his days, Boris would have to live with not knowing if they would have patched the argument up. But was his sorrow all an act? If so, it was a good one.

'What did you do instead?' he asked.

'I make sure everything ready for show. Then I come back here.'

'Do you remember what time that was?'

Boris thought for a moment. 'Half past eleven maybe. I stay here until it is time for show.'

'Did you not go to eat lunch?'

'No. I do not eat before show.' He smiled wanly. 'Nadia will tell you I eat like bear after.'

'When did you last see Tatiana?'

'Before I come back to tent. She is on high wire, making check.'

'Was Izabella there too?'

Boris frowned. 'No, I did not see her before show.'

If Izabella made her check at twelve, that was plausible. 'Is the main tent usually deserted at lunchtime?'

'I think so.'

'I couldn't help hearing that you and Nadia were having a disagreement over something just now. May I ask what it was?'

The flush on Boris's cheeks, which had been fading, returned. De Silva hoped he had not overstepped the mark. But then Boris shrugged. 'Nothing is right for her today,' he said bitterly. 'She is sad for Tatiana Petrovna and Alexei Ivanovich, but what can I do?'

Briefly, de Silva caught a glimpse of a little boy who wanted his nurse to comfort, not scold him. 'She say maybe Izabella innocent and I do nothing for her,' Boris went on. 'I tell her Izabella safe with you, but she is not satisfied.'

Nadia had not seemed particularly concerned over Izabella's situation. The story didn't ring true, but de Silva played along with it.

'Please assure her that Miss Rabach is being well treated. Indeed, she seems to accept that for the moment, she is better off where she is.'

Boris raised an eyebrow. 'I tell Nadia; if she speak to me again.'

'Good.'

'You have more questions?'

'Not for the present. Thank you for your time.'

* * *

Outside, de Silva debated going to look for Prasanna and Gordo but decided against it. It would do his sergeant good to take charge of the inquiries. Instead, he went to find out if the undertakers had been to collect Alexei's and Tatiana's bodies. He decided they must have done so, because the tent where they had been the previous night was deserted.

Afterwards, he strolled away from the tented area and over the track towards the racecourse buildings. As he walked, he mulled over what he had learnt. If Boris wasn't telling the truth about spending time alone in his tent, he'd had the opportunity to kill Alexei and string up his body to look as if it had been suicide.

Once more, he fell to thinking about Izabella. She was the most likely candidate for the role of Boris's accomplice, both from the point of view of ability and of motive – a promise of Tatiana's place in the act – but trapping her into a confession was going to be difficult. Even though their last encounter had been quite amicable, with her temperament that could change in a flash. He doubted she would give up any secrets in a hurry.

At the parking area near the racecourse entrance, the spot where he had left the Morris was no longer in the shade, and it was broiling in the car. He decided to find somewhere cooler. Wandering towards the stables, he heard the sound of hammer on metal and followed it.

Near the main barn, a brazier had been lit; the sulphurous smell of the glowing coals made de Silva's nose prickle. Kumar was bent down by the back legs of one of the horses. He held up a hoof and was hammering on a new shoe, whistling as he did so. De Silva waited until he had finished before he called out to him. Kumar looked up; for a moment, de Silva thought he saw a guarded look in his eyes but then it vanished.

'Can I help you?'

De Silva shook his head. 'I'm waiting for my sergeant. I was just looking for somewhere in the shade.'

Kumar gestured to the barn. 'It is cooler in there, and comfortable, if you will sit on a bale of straw.'

De Silva grinned. 'I've sat on worse.'

Kumar chuckled.

De Silva followed him as he led the horse into the barn. He slapped it on the rump, and it ambled off. 'Horseshoes wear down quickly on your roads,' he remarked as it started to pull straw from a nearby net. 'The horses often need new ones.'

'Lucky for the circus that you inherited your father's skills.'

'Ah, you have a good memory. Yes, it was useful that I was able to help Alexei.' He sighed. 'I don't know what Boris will do with the horses. Maybe he'll sell them. I can help the other riders to look after them for now, but the act won't be the same without Alexei.'

'It would be a shame if they have to be sold. I'm sure your audiences enjoy seeing them.'

'They do, but there's a lot of work. Unless Boris finds someone like Alexei to take charge, it will be hard. Now, please excuse me. The rest of the horses need to be brought in before it gets dark.'

De Silva followed him out of the barn, and they parted company. He returned to the Morris and waited in the swiftly gathering dusk until Prasanna came hurrying into the parking area. 'I'm sorry to have kept you waiting for so long, sir.'

'How did you get on?'

'Slowly, I'm afraid. I've not spoken to all the people I'd hoped to yet. Gordo talks a lot, and he likes to joke with everyone. It was hard to make him hurry.'

'Did he give you his opinion on the case?'

'Yes, sir. He believes that Alexei committed suicide. When I suggested that Tatiana's fall might not be an accident, he asked if you thought Izabella had a hand in it. He said she didn't like Tatiana, but he didn't know. The idea of her being close to Alexei or Boris just made him laugh.'

Prasanna frowned. 'Oddly, he didn't seem worried about Alexei's death, or Tatiana's. In fact, he said it might be a good thing for the circus in the long run, because they were always quarrelling. Boris and Alexei often argued too, although they usually made it up afterwards. He said that if Boris can find new people who are less trouble everyone will be happier.'

'Did he have anything else to say about Boris?'

'He hinted that Boris once had a drinking problem. It made him bad-tempered and affected his work.'

'I see. Well, what did you find out from other people?'

'Everyone we spoke to confirmed what Izabella told you about her morning, apart from the time she was going for a walk alone, when no one saw her. She hadn't stayed long to eat her lunch. A lot of people saw Tatiana. She checked the equipment and spent time talking to other performers. She ate lunch with them then went to her tent to get ready for the show.'

'And Alexei?'

'No one mentioned seeing him.'

'Boris?'

'Plenty of people vouched for the fact he was working

in the main tent for the first few hours of the morning, but after that no one saw him.'

'Did anyone think it was odd?'

'No. Unless there are any problems to attend to, he usually choses to be on his own for a few hours before a performance.'

'Hmm. That accords with what he told me. Anything else of interest?'

'No, sir, except that we passed the tent belonging to the snake charmer, Kumar. It's where he keeps his snakes.'

De Silva would have described that experience as alarming rather than interesting.

'He wasn't there, so Gordo took me inside for a quick look. I hadn't expected there to be so many, sir; far more than we saw in the act. Some are extremely beautiful.'

His skin crawling at the image of a writhing mass of sibilant reptilian life, de Silva hastily opened the driver's door. 'Jump in; it's time we got back to town. We'll have to come up here later for you to finish your inquiries.'

* * *

He dropped Prasanna at his house before going on to the police station. It would do Nadar no harm to remain on guard duty for a bit longer. To his surprise, the constable was not as downcast at the news as he had expected.

'Now the lady is quiet, sir,' he said with a grin, 'it is more peaceful here than at home.'

De Silva chuckled. 'I'm glad to hear there's some advantage. Has there been any news from Hatton about this burglary while I've been out?'

'No, sir.' Nadar hesitated.

'What is it, Constable?'

'If you are staying for a while, sir, may I go to find something to eat? I did not like to leave the lady alone.'

'Of course. You had better fetch food for her as well.' De Silva reached into his pocket for some money. 'Here, take this. Oh, and whilst you're about it, I want a note delivered to Doctor Hebden's surgery. It's on my desk.'

'Yes, sir.'

While Nadar was gone, there was no sound from the cells. De Silva didn't risk going to investigate. At the moment, there was nothing more he had to say to Izabella Rabach; best to let sleeping dogs lie. Although, he mused gloomily, her cooperative mood was not guaranteed to last. If she insisted on leaving, his choice would fall between charging her, which might necessitate arresting Boris too, or letting her go. Neither prospect was appealing.

Nadar returned with enough food to feed a small army. De Silva smelled enticing aromas of coriander, cumin, and cardamom coming from the tin containers. Lightly charred naan bread, shining with ghee, poked out from the top of a brown paper bag. If his charge continued to cause no trouble, the night that stretched before Nadar might be relatively pleasant. He left him to it and drove home.

* * *

Ensconced in his favourite chair in the drawing room, with Bella on his lap and a whisky at his elbow, life seemed much improved, although he wondered why Jane seemed rather distant as he recounted the details of his conversation with Archie.

'Have I done something wrong?' he asked eventually.

'Nothing at all. Why do you ask?'

De Silva regarded her shrewdly. 'Because I know that expression.'

'Well, if you must know, at church everyone was talking about this burglary on Friday at the de Vere plantation. I was surprised you hadn't mentioned it to me.'

'Ah, that's what it is. I hadn't mentioned it, my love, because I only heard about it from Archie this morning. I went to the station to question Izabella Rabach after that, and then up to the circus. I'm sorry if you thought I was hiding something from you.'

She smiled. 'I forgive you.'

'I spoke to Singh, and luckily, he doesn't appear to need any backup. I've enough on my plate at the moment.'

'I know you have, dear,' said Jane. 'I'm sorry I doubted you. How did you get on at the circus?'

'I wanted Prasanna to find out about our suspects' movements yesterday morning and pick up any other information that might be useful, so I sent him off with one of the clowns, a man called Gordo, to interpret for him. Gordo speaks a reasonable amount of English, and I was warned that most of the circus people only speak Russian. Prasanna didn't manage to talk to everyone, so I'll have to take him up there again, but so far he has established that Tatiana was about the place as usual, but no one saw Boris after the first few hours. After she made her check at twelve o'clock, Izabella spent a short time eating lunch then went off on her own. Alexei wasn't in evidence at all. That means that the only person who had any idea where he was yesterday was Kumar, when he helped him with the horses first thing. Also, the main tent was probably deserted at lunchtime.'

'So, if it wasn't suicide, there were several hours during which Boris might have killed his brother, and while the main tent was deserted, and she claimed to have gone for a walk, Izabella could have tampered with the wire unnoticed.'

'Yes. Prasanna asked Gordo if he thought she was close to either Alexei or Boris, but the idea only seemed to amuse him. That doesn't mean we should discount it yet, of course. Gordo also mentioned that Alexei and Boris often argued, as did Alexei and Tatiana. When I went to Boris's tent to talk to him he was with Nadia, the wardrobe mistress. The two of them were quarrelling over something, but I didn't understand what they were saying. She was obviously still angry when she left.'

'Did you mention it when you talked to him?'

'Yes. He passed it off as being due to her sorrow over Tatiana and Alexei's deaths. Nothing he did was right. There was also something about him not doing enough to help Izabella, but that seemed odd. When I spoke to Nadia about Izabella, she didn't appear to be particularly anxious about her fate. Like Nadia, Boris said that he was sure Alexei had committed suicide because of his difficulties with Tatiana. But unlike her, he hotly denied Alexei would have done anything to harm her beforehand.'

'How did he explain the grease on the wire then?'

'He suggested it might be Izabella after all, or one of his people had made a mistake and was lying about it.'

He drank some of his whisky. 'You know, I still regret missing David Hebden. I should have asked him sooner to come back to examine the body.'

'I'm not sure that it would have made a difference,' said Jane consolingly. 'You often say he's not able to be very precise about a time of death.'

'But it might have helped to remove some uncertainty.'

Bella rearranged herself in his lap and he stroked her. She purred contentedly.

Jane glanced around the room. 'Goodness, where's Billy?'

'I'm not sure.'

'I'll take a look outside. I hope he hasn't wandered away.' She patted Bella's sleek head. 'It's just as well you don't have the same adventurous streak as your brother.'

On the verandah, she found Billy crouched flat on the wooden floor, his green eyes intently scanning a shadowy corner. 'He's spotted something,' Jane called back. 'I hope it's not a mouse.'

De Silva yawned. 'I'll come and see.'

As he stood up, Bella jumped from his lap then trotted out to the verandah. There was a flicker in the shadows; Billy pounced and missed. A lizard darted down the steps to the garden and into the safety of a flowerbed.

De Silva scratched Billy behind the ears. 'Better luck next time, young man. But I'd prefer it if you would concentrate your efforts on any rats and mice that may be around. Lizards perform a useful function.'

'Inside now, both of you,' said Jane.

Billy scooted through the door to the drawing room, Bella following at a more leisurely pace.

'The Applebys were at church today, and George asked me about these two,' said Jane. 'He recommended we have them neutered if we're not planning to breed from them. At least have Billy done as it's a straightforward operation.'

Involuntarily, de Silva winced.

'He said that it makes male cats less inclined to stray, which may be a good thing with Billy. What do you think?'

'I suppose we should take his advice, at least about Billy. After all, he is the government veterinary advisor.'

'And Bella?'

'I'd like to know more about the risks.'

'I agree.'

'Would George Appleby carry out the operation?'

'He offered to. Emerald gave me his home number. I'll give him a call.'

'Fine.'

After dinner, they listened to music on the gramophone, but de Silva's thoughts kept straying to the case. Was he allowing his annoyance that he hadn't called David Hebden back sooner to colour his judgment on whether Alexei's suicide was genuine? He didn't really have a lot to go on where Boris and Izabella were concerned.

The last notes of Elgar's *Enigma Variations* died away. It was a piece he had grown to love; by turns moving, lyrical, rousing, majestic, confident, and playful. To him, its popularity explained something about the nature of the British and the love of their country that their stiff upper lips concealed.

'Would you like to listen to something else?' asked Jane.

'No, I think my head is filled with enough music for one night.'

She smiled. 'Elgar does have that effect. His music has so many lovely melodies.' She looked at the clock. 'You look tired, dear. I might read for a while, but why don't you get to bed? I'll try not to wake you when I come in.'

He put Bella onto the floor. 'Perhaps I will.'

If he stayed up, he would only want to talk about the case and distract Jane, who had already picked up her book. He couldn't see the cover, but it was sure to be a detective novel that she would enjoy all the more if it had a fiendishly complicated plot. Perhaps he ought to accept that wasn't what he had on his hands in Nuala, and the case was the tragedy of a beautiful girl who had paid a terrible price for her thoughtless behaviour, and a young man who had let his passions get the better of him.

In the bedroom, he opened the window a little to freshen the air and got ready for bed. He had been sure it would take him a long time to fall asleep, but as the soft, rustling sounds of nocturnal animals and insects drifted from the garden and a light breeze stirred the curtains, thoughts of the case faded. Drowsily, he heard an owl hoot in the garden. By the time Jane came to bed, he was sound asleep.

CHAPTER 7

The next morning, he collected Prasanna and they drove back up to the racecourse. When they went to find Gordo, de Silva was pleased to see that Boris was in the circus ring watching the dance group. He had been thinking on the way up that if there was an opportunity to search his and Alexei's tents, it was something he ought to get on with.

'They practise new act,' said Gordo. 'When we move on, there will be more dancing in show until boss find new people to take place of Alexei Ivanovich and Tatiana Petrovna.'

So, Boris didn't plan to offer Tatiana's starring role to Izabella.

Leaving Prasanna and Gordo to carry on with questioning the rest of the circus people, he went quietly to Boris's tent. Urbane as he was in his ringmaster's costume, Boris's taste in furnishings was spartan. In a screened-off area that de Silva had not seen into on his previous visit, he found an unmade camp bed, a chair, and a few clothes on a rail with a row of shoes underneath. There were also an empty trunk and another smaller one containing account ledgers, circus posters, handbills, programmes, and books of tickets. Beneath it all, he found a cloth bag containing a document sealed with red wax. The paper crackled as he smoothed it out.

It was Ivan Goncharov's will. Dated after the family had left Russia, fortunately, it was written in English. De Silva presumed that Goncharov had thought it would be a more useful language than Russian. He scanned the provisions before returning it to the bag. Nadia had been right; Ivan had left the circus to his sons in equal shares, with the proviso that they looked after Tatiana. If one of them wanted to leave, or died, the other would be entitled to the whole business. In the case of death, the survivor must provide for his brother's widow and children, if any.

Also in the bag was a packet of photographs. The first one he picked up was a grainy, sepia portrait of a stern-looking couple posed beside an aspidistra; the lady sat on a high-backed chair with the man standing behind her, one hand resting on her shoulder. De Silva assumed they were Ivan Goncharov and his wife. Other photographs were informal. They showed children who he guessed to be Boris, Alexei, and Tatiana. In some they played in a garden with a long, low house in the background; in others, they rode ponies.

The only touch of luxury in the tent was a mahogany washstand. On its shelves were ranged an assortment of bottles and jars containing shampoo, rouge, lotions, and toilet water. There was soap scented with sandalwood, a tortoiseshell comb, a silver-backed brush, scissors for trimming hair or paring nails, polish and brushes for shining shoes, and stiff brushes for clothes.

The last thing he found was a jar of pomade. Remembering how Boris's hair had been slicked back when he acted as ringmaster, de Silva unscrewed the lid. He studied the thick, viscous substance. Could this be what had been smeared on the wire? He sniffed it; it had a strong, sweetish scent that reminded him of vanilla. It was not the smell of the greasy substance he and Hebden had found.

He replaced the lid and returned to the living area. On the table where he and Boris had sat the previous day, there was a coffee pot with a mess of damp grounds in the bottom, a plate with a few crumbs of bread and a smear of jam on it, and another with a curl of orange rind and a knife. De Silva smelled a citrusy tang. Clearly, no one had been to tidy Boris's quarters yet. He must keep a sharp ear out and be ready to move quickly if he heard anyone approach. Luckily, he had noticed there was a way out from the sleeping area as well as the main one.

On a folding table doing duty as a desk were piles of papers and letters, along with writing equipment, and two oil lamps. Carefully, he removed the rubber band around the letters and looked through them. Some had to do with bookings for the circus and others acknowledged orders for supplies of food and fuel at future stops. There were also contracts with the circus performers and circus hands.

Hearing a sound outside, he quickly tidied everything and hurried back to the sleeping area. A moment later, he stole a look around the flap dividing the two areas and saw that a servant had come in. The man put down the fresh linen he carried and began to collect up the dirty crockery. There was a chance to escape in time before he came to make the bed.

Cautiously, de Silva peered out of the sleeping area's exit. There was no one in sight. As he was about to step outside, a glint caught his eye. He stooped and saw that there was an empty vodka bottle on the ground. It must have rolled out from under the canvas when he opened the tent flap. There was another one tucked behind it. Was vodka what had caused the argument between Nadia and Boris? Sadly, he shook his head. The circus had enough problems. It would be a great pity if Boris's old habit had resurfaced to add to them.

He glanced at his watch. Prasanna was probably still busy. There was time to find Alexei's tent and take a look around. He hoped not to be disturbed, but if his luck ran out he would have to say he was making a routine check.

In contrast to his brother's quarters, Alexei's contained no business papers or letters; in fact, there was nothing to show that he was joint owner of the business. It seemed Boris was responsible for the lion's share of administration and planning. The tent had obviously been shared with Tatiana, for women's clothes were everywhere: a plethora of frocks, blouses, fashionable trousers, high-heeled shoes, and hats. There was also silk underwear, and nightgowns in shades of ecru and shell pink. De Silva caught the musky scents of rose and patchouli and had the uncomfortable feeling that he was intruding on the dead couple's privacy. The dressing table mirror had numerous photographs of Tatiana in stage costume tucked into its gilt frame. There were also some of Alexei with his horses. None of Tatiana's stage costumes were in evidence; he assumed they were looked after by Nadia.

Taking care to put everything back in the same disorder as he had found it, de Silva went through untidy drawers and trunks. There was no sign of a suicide note. It didn't prove anything, but in his experience, people who took their own lives usually left something. Had Alexei omitted to do so because he was sure Tatiana would be dead by the time his body was found, and she was the only person he cared about? If Boris was innocent, it would surely increase his pain that his brother had no last words for him.

De Silva had finished his search and was at a good distance from Alexei's tent when Boris emerged from the main one. He raised a hand and started to walk in de Silva's direction. 'Good morning, Inspector, I see your officer with Gordo.'

De Silva nodded. 'Prasanna came up to make routine inquiries in accordance with my instructions.'

'I understand. Does this take long?'

'I'm going to look for him now, so I'll find out, but I imagine he won't need very much more time.'

'Good. We give no show today, and soon, I hope, we move on.' He looked sad. 'But first, we must have funeral for Alexei and Tatiana.'

De Silva was relieved that Boris hadn't asked what he had been doing while Prasanna was carrying out the so-called routine inquiries. 'Of course,' he replied. 'If you like, I can introduce you to the local vicar.' Boris looked blank. De Silva searched his mind for another way of describing Reverend Peters and came up with the word priest.

'Ah, I see,' said Boris. 'Alexei and Tatiana belonged to our Russian church.'

'Our priest is the vicar of the English church here – we have no Russian one – but I'm sure he will do his best to help. He's a good man.'

Boris nodded. 'Thank you.' He paused. 'You let Izabella go now? When we leave here, I want to take her with us.'

De Silva hesitated. His doubts about the case against Izabella had continued to grow since the previous night. She was a bitter woman, but was there really enough malice in her to make her deliberately cause a fatal accident? And surely, if Boris was the culprit, he could have found a way of getting rid of his brother without harming Tatiana. Wouldn't that have been the better way forward? He wouldn't have to lose his star performer, and there was always a chance that a bereft Tatiana would turn to him for comfort. The pomade he had just found might have made him change his mind, but then there was the different scent to consider. Maybe he really was looking for complications where there were none. He considered the possibility that Alexei had been a more calculating man than he had originally believed and had used some substance of his own to grease the wire that they might never find.

Before he gave Boris his answer, however, there was one last thing he wanted to do.

'I'd like to see inside Izabella's tent before I decide.'

'Very well.'

The tent was by far the smallest de Silva had been into. Searching it didn't take him long, and he found nothing suspicious. As Boris waited at the entrance, he made his decision.

'I'm satisfied that she played no part in the accident,' he said. 'If you believe you can keep her safe, I will let her go.'

Boris gave him a searching look. 'Then one of my people make mistake.' He clenched one fist. 'I ask questions; I find them.'

'If there are questions to ask, please leave that to me, sir,' de Silva said calmly. He hesitated. 'But I'm afraid you must accept the possibility that this has nothing to do with your people. It may have been your brother's work.'

Anger flashed in Boris's eyes, and de Silva had to stop himself from taking a step backwards. It was replaced by abject sorrow.

'This is hard for me to hear.' There was a catch in Boris's voice, and it was difficult to believe his sadness was feigned. De Silva felt a rush of pity for him. With Alexei and Tatiana gone, Boris would probably have no one he was close to except Nadia.

'I'll go and see if my sergeant is ready yet,' he said. 'Then I suggest you follow me to the station and collect Izabella.'

* * *

Prasanna still needed to speak to a few people, so de Silva agreed to return for him. With Boris following in one of the circus trucks, he drove back to town. Nadar's obvious relief at his arrival was briefly wiped from his face when Boris walked into the station too. Perhaps he thought there was going to be an ugly scene.

De Silva gave him a reassuring smile. 'I'm releasing Miss Rabach. Mr Goncharov will be taking her back to the circus and seeing to it that she's safe. Go and fetch her, please.'

Nadar hesitated.

'Well? What are you waiting for? She won't bite.'

Izabella came out from her cell with a haughty expression on her face. She clearly felt that she had been unjustly treated. She refused to meet de Silva's eyes and stalked out with Boris behind her. He suspected that it would be the last he saw of her.

* * *

Back at the circus, Prasanna was ready for him.

'Anything to report, Sergeant?' he asked on the way back to town.

'Nothing more than I found out yesterday, sir.'

'I promised to speak to Reverend Peters about funeral arrangements for Alexei and Tatiana. As Boris Goncharov hopes to move on soon, I'll telephone Peters as soon as possible. Of course, the coroner's office will need our report and Doctor Hebden's, which will have to wait until he returns from his fishing trip, before the bodies are released for burial.'

'Do you mean you don't suspect Boris or Izabella any longer, sir?'

De Silva relaxed back in his seat, one hand on the steering wheel and the other on his knee. 'That's right. I believe that Izabella is telling the truth. And if Boris had wanted his brother dead, there would have been easier ways of achieving it that didn't involve losing his star performer. Since the circus tent was empty for a period of time during which no one knew where Alexei was, he had the opportunity to tamper with the wire himself.'

They drove on. To de Silva, the breeze seemed more refreshing than usual and the colour of the trees lining the road more vivid. A flock of green parrots rose from a field as they passed. With amusement, he noticed that Prasanna's head was nodding. The young man must be tired. When they arrived at the police station, de Silva gave him and Nadar the rest of the day off. 'And there's no need to hurry here in the morning,' he added.

They didn't wait for him to change his mind. Left alone, he wrote up his report from his own notes and those that Prasanna had left with him. When he had read it over and made a few corrections, he placed it in a folder and labelled it.

He was about to put on his jacket when he noticed that the latest digest of crime reports from Kandy lay on his desk. He looked at his watch. Maybe he would deal with them before he went home. Going out to the back, he made himself a cup of tea, took it to his office and settled down to read.

The electric fan suspended from the ceiling thrummed rhythmically. It wasn't long before his mind started to wander, but he blinked and shook himself. There was only one more page; the sooner he finished it, the sooner he would feel justified in going home. It would be pleasant to spend the last part of the afternoon in the garden and then enjoy a whisky on the verandah with Jane before dinner. He wondered what her opinion on the outcome of the case would be. Somehow, he doubted that she would be surprised. From their last discussion, he suspected that she had already come to the same conclusion that he had now reached. He smiled; as was not infrequently the case, he could probably have saved himself some time if he'd listened to her in the first place.

He turned his attention back to the last page of the digest. There had been four robberies recently – the one at the de Vere plantation, and three at plantations near Kandy. In each case, a large quantity of valuable jewellery had been stolen. All the break-ins had been at night when the families were away and only a few servants left to watch the house. In every case, they had gone to bed and had claimed not to have heard anything. Like the de Veres' servants, the others had been trusted employees with long service.

De Silva wondered whether he should telephone Singh to ask if there had been any developments, but on reflection, as Singh had promised to keep him informed, he decided to wait for a while. It would be advisable, however, to notify the wealthier families in the Nuala area of the need to take extra security measures, at least until the gang had been caught. Archie might prefer the advice to come from the Residence so he drafted a note with a suggested message that he would drop in on his way home.

He drained the last of his tea and swatted a fly that had settled on a few grains of sugar he'd spilt in the saucer. Unless it had come in when he opened the door, the window must be open a crack. He went to check and pulled the handle down firmly. Back at his desk, he straightened the papers. He would leave them out on the desk to remind him to telephone Singh at some point if he didn't hear from him. The thought prompted the recollection that he had promised Boris Goncharov to speak to Reverend Peters.

It was Mrs Peters who answered the telephone. 'I'm afraid my husband is out visiting a sick parishioner,' she said. 'Is there anything I can do to help?'

He explained the situation and heard her give a sympathetic click of the tongue. 'How terribly sad. And their religion is Russian Orthodox, you say. I'm not sure what the church's policy is on that.' An anxious note entered her voice. 'Especially with the complication of the manner of the poor man's death.'

De Silva frowned. He hadn't considered the church's

attitude to suicide. It came back to him that, irrespective of the different religions, that was likely to cause a problem if Boris wanted his brother buried in consecrated ground.

'But I'm sure Ambrose will do his best for them,' Mrs Peters went on. 'I'll ask him to call you as soon as he comes in.'

'Thank you. I'm leaving for the day shortly, but he can reach me at home.'

CHAPTER 8

Prasanna climbed the stairs to the apartment he shared with his wife, Kuveni, and their daughter, Anika. He called out as he opened the door, and she came running to meet him. He swung her up into his arms and hugged her.

'Have you missed me?'

She nodded as her mother appeared from the direction of their small kitchen. 'You're home early. Is everything alright?'

'Yes, the case is finished. He gave us the rest of the day off.'

The previous evening, he had already told her about what had happened after Tatiana's accident. Now he explained about Izabella's release and the conclusion de Silva had come to.

Kuveni raised an eyebrow. 'So, Nadar no longer needs to guard this ferocious lady.'

'I expect he'll wildly exaggerate the difficulties he's had,' said Prasanna with a grin.

'You must allow him to boast a little.'

'If you say so. Now, I must go and wash. Have we anything to eat? I've had no lunch, and I'm starving.'

'I bought vegetables at the bazaar this morning and made curry. I'll cook some rice to go with it. It won't take long.'

A short time later, washed and dressed in a clean sarong and shirt, he sat down to eat with Anika perched on his lap. He broke off a piece of naan bread to give her and she munched it happily.

'I saw your mother at the bazaar,' said Kuveni, turning from the stove where she was stirring something in a pan. 'She complained that she never sees you. You should go and visit her when you've eaten.'

Prasanna sighed. He had been looking forward to spending the rest of the day quietly.

'She gets lonely without your father. Just go for a little while. You can take her some of the butter cake I made this morning.'

'Alright.'

After he had finished his meal, he lifted Anika off his lap. 'Daddy has to go out for a while. You stay here with your mother and play with your toys.'

The little girl's forehead wrinkled.

'When something doesn't suit her, she looks just like you,' said Kuveni with a laugh.

She handed him the parcel of cake, and he kissed her cheek. 'I won't be long.'

* * *

There were streaks of crimson and gold in the sky. Soon, with the speed it always did in the tropics, darkness would fall. Prasanna passed people trudging home from work or sitting outside their doors smoking and chatting as the heat of the day faded. At the bazaar, many of the stallholders had packed up and gone home, leaving unsold vegetables and fruit on the ground to be picked up by anyone needy enough to want them. There was already a faintly putrid smell in the air. Two skinny dogs snapped and snarled at each other as they circled a puddle of broken eggs.

The part of the city where Prasanna's mother lived

lacked electricity. The narrow streets were lit only by the oil lamps that some of the inhabitants hung by their doors. He moved from one pool of light to another, alert for the sound of footsteps. The neighbourhood was perfectly safe in the daytime but could be less so at night. As he kept telling his mother, who often forgot to lock her front door, it was best to be cautious. At the door, he tried the handle. Good, she had remembered to lock up this evening. He knocked and waited for her to come.

She was a tall, striking lady, whose dark hair was always glossy and sweet smelling with scented oil. Her olive sari was made of good quality material; a fine chain with a golden medallion glowed against her skin. 'So, you have found time to visit your mother at last.'

'I've been busy, Mother.'

She gave him a stern look then laughed. 'I'm teasing. I know you are busy. Come in.'

He followed her to the kitchen, where there was a mound of chopped vegetables on the table. A pot of soup simmered on the stove.

'Kuveni tells me your inspector gives you a lot more responsibility these days.'

'He does.' He put the package he carried on the table. 'She sent you some butter cake.'

'That was kind of her. Will you thank her for me? And how is my granddaughter? She looked thin when I saw her with Kuveni this morning.'

'You mustn't worry about her. Anika eats plenty of food. It's just that now she can run about, she's not as plump as she used to be.'

'I suppose, you were a skinny child.'

Prasanna looked down at his belly. It was still flat, but he was not as thin as he had been when he and Kuveni married.

'Now you're here, you must eat.'

He knew better than to argue with his mother, so he found room for a bowl of the thick soup she had made, a delicious creamy mixture of sweet potato and coconut, spiced with ginger and cumin. She insisted he follow it with a large slice of Kuveni's butter cake. Afterwards he fixed the bracket on a shelf that had come loose, went to borrow tools from a neighbour to repair a pipe under the kitchen sink that was leaking, and drank several cups of the tea that his mother made him.

By the time he started for home, the evening was half over. Once more he was careful to keep an eye on the other people who were out. In one street, he saw a shadow by the wall and tensed, ready to defend himself, but it was only a cat crouched in the gutter. It hissed, and he realised it was guarding a fish skeleton. 'Don't worry,' he said as it dragged off its prize. 'I'm not interested in your dinner.'

He was about to carry on walking when a man came out of the next side street. He hesitated for a moment, and in the light of a nearby oil lamp, Prasanna caught a glimpse of him before he walked briskly away in the other direction. Something about him was familiar. He had already put a good distance between them, but curiosity made Prasanna want to find out what he was up to.

Fifty yards ahead, the man turned into another side street, but Prasanna decided not to follow. He knew the area well enough to remember there was a shortcut that would bring him out close to the other end of it. Quickly, he made his way there and waited. A moment later, the man came into sight. As he passed the place where Prasanna hid in the shadows, Prasanna saw the man's face. It was Kumar, the snake charmer. What was he doing in town late at night? Prasanna waited for him to get well ahead before he tailed him.

The part of town they came to was one that Prasanna rarely visited. It was certainly not an area where he would want Kuveni or his mother to go. Even he was doubtful of the wisdom of being there alone at night, but he was determined to see where Kumar was heading. Two men were coming towards him now, obviously the worse for drink. When they came level with Kumar, one of them grabbed him by the arm and pushed his face close to Kumar's own. Prasanna tensed. If the men tried to beat Kumar up, as a policeman he ought to intervene, but that would give the game away.

The man who held Kumar by the sleeve seemed to be demanding money. His companion, who had hung back at first, started pawing at his shoulder. Prasanna was on the point of going to help him and taking the consequences when, with lightning speed, the snake charmer broke free of the man holding his sleeve; jabbing his elbow into the second man's ribs, he seized both men by their collars, and cracked their foreheads together.

The second man doubled over, howling with pain, but the one who had made the first move recovered, raising his fists ready to fight. Swiftly, Kumar landed a punch to his chest and another to his stomach. The man reeled backwards into his friend before regaining his balance. Grabbing him by the collar, he dragged him away.

Coolly, Kumar watched them go, smoothing down his clothing and slicking a hand through his dark hair. Prasanna heard him laugh quietly as if the encounter had amused, rather than alarmed, him. Even though he was not a big man, thought Prasanna, he had certainly needed no help to defend himself.

Even more cautiously than before the incident, for he had no desire to receive the same treatment as the would-be thieves, Prasanna shadowed Kumar until they reached a part of town that even in daylight he would be wary of entering alone. Kumar seemed to be looking for a particular house. Eventually, he stopped at a door and knocked.

A few moments passed before a head poked out of an upstairs window. There was a muffled exchange of conversation and then the head disappeared. A few more moments passed before the door opened and Kumar stepped inside. A man came out and looked up and down the street then, apparently satisfied that Kumar had not been followed, went back inside and closed the door.

Prasanna wondered whether he should wait until Kumar came out, but after ten minutes, he decided not to. There was no name to identify the street, as was the case in many areas away from the centre of Nuala, but some of the frontages of the buildings, crumbling as they were, had distinctive decoration in the form of tiled panels on the walls. He would remember the way. The boss would be interested to hear about this. Hopefully, they would be able to find out why Kumar had chosen to visit such a seedy part of town.

CHAPTER 9

'Hello!'

De Silva walked into the hall at Sunnybank and listened for Jane's voice, but there was silence. She was not in the drawing room, but the door to the verandah was open. Expecting to see her there, he stepped outside, but it too was deserted.

'Jane!'

Still no answer. Perhaps she had gone for a walk around the garden taking the kittens with her. He headed across the lawn, yet by the time he reached the far boundary, there was still no sign of them. The only occupant of the vegetable garden was a mynah bird. It cocked its head, showing off its distinctive yellow bill and the splash of yellow around its eyes, before going back to tugging at a worm that it had found in a patch of recently dug-over soil.

Puzzled, and becoming somewhat anxious, de Silva returned to the house. The only place he had not looked was the area at the back of the bungalow where the servants lived, and the cooking and laundry was done. Perhaps they would know where Jane had got to.

He had nearly reached the back yard when Jane came around the corner, almost colliding with him.

'Shanti! Thank goodness you're home. Perhaps Bella will come down for you. Billy found his own way, but I think she's too frightened to move.'

'Come down from where?' asked de Silva apprehensively. Hopefully, nothing too high; he was not fond of heights.

'The roof of the washhouse. Delisha went out to fetch in the laundry and found them playing hide and seek around the sheets. They made her jump, so she screamed and that alarmed them. They ran up the tree that one end of the line's tied to and jumped from there onto the roof.'

'I'll come and see.'

In the yard outside the washhouse, Billy was sitting in the sun, calmly grooming a paw. De Silva looked up at the roof and saw Bella close to the edge, precariously balanced with her back arched and her paws wedged against the edge of a broken tile. Delisha and the cook stood below, the cook holding out a bowl of scraps to try to entice her down. Anif, their gardener, hovered nearby holding a ladder.

'Anif tried to get to her with that,' said Jane. 'But she only ran further up the roof to where she is now. He offered to climb up after her, but I told him not to. The tiles are old and brittle and sure to break under his weight. Perhaps if you go up the ladder and call her, she'll come to you.'

De Silva looked at the distance from the ground to the edge of the roof. Even though it was only one storey up, it was further than he was comfortable with.

But then he looked again at Bella; she gave a piteous meow.

'Set up the ladder,' he said to Anif.

When the ladder was in place, Anif held it steady, and de Silva put his foot on the bottom rung. 'I wouldn't do this for anyone else,' he muttered under his breath as he began to climb. At the top, his fingers met the rough, warm surface of the clay tiles. His eyes met Bella's jade ones; they seemed larger than usual in her little black face. He swallowed hard, trying to rid his throat of the dryness that had invaded it. Cautiously letting go of the ladder with one hand, he stretched it out towards Bella.

'Come on, little one. It's not far; I'll catch you.'

Concentrating on Bella and forgetting where he was, he shifted his weight. The ladder lurched, and his foot almost slipped off the rung it was on. His stomach somersaulted. Bella continued to watch him, her tail waving slowly from side to side. She let out another plaintive meow.

Suddenly, there was a raucous cry and something flapped close to his cheek. Out of the corner of his eye, he saw the slate-blue plumage of a house crow. Its beady eyes glinted menacingly. Opening its sharp, powerful beak, it cawed again, and despite his attempts to shoo it away, started to hop in Bella's direction. His heart thudded. The crow was larger than Bella. He tried to remember what crows ate. Bella hissed as it came closer, then a paw darted out, swiping at the bird. Unprepared, it let out a squawk, took off from the roof and flew into the tree where the washing line was tied.

De Silva chuckled. His little girl was not so timid after all. Calmly, she started to pick her way down the tiles until she reached him. Nuzzling his cheek, she meowed again, but this time, the tone of the meow was contented. Risking letting go with one hand again, de Silva tucked her under his arm and began his descent. If nothing else, he reflected, the escapade had provided a distraction from any doubts about his decision over Izabella.

* * *

'I knew she'd come down for you,' said Jane with a smile. He leant back in his chair on the verandah and took a sip of his whisky. He felt he had earned it this evening.

'Did you have to take her back to the circus?' she asked when he explained about Izabella's release and the events leading up to it.

'Boris came to the police station and fetched her. Unless he makes a complaint to Archie, which I doubt Archie would take much notice of anyway, I expect I'll hear no more about it.'

'I'm sure you made the right decision.'

'I hope so.' He raised an eyebrow. 'Boris intends to move the circus on as soon as possible, so I haven't much time to change my mind. All he wants to do before they go is hold the funerals for Tatiana and Alexei. I spoke to Reverend Peters' wife earlier this afternoon and left a message for him. I hope he'll telephone me this evening. It may be complicated by the fact that their religion was Russian Orthodox. There may also be a religious problem if Alexei's death was a suicide.'

'I had forgotten that might be the case,' said Jane with a sigh. 'But I expect Reverend Peters will try to find a way of holding a funeral service of some kind, even if it can't be the full one. At least it might comfort Boris and the other circus people who were fond of them.'

'Let's hope so. By the way, do you remember I told you that I heard Boris and Nadia having an argument?'

'Yes.'

'Something the clown mentioned to Prasanna might be the clue to what that was about.'

He explained about Boris's drinking problem in the past and the empty vodka bottles outside his sleeping quarters.

'So, Nadia may have found out he was drinking again, and that was why they were arguing,' said Jane with a sigh. 'I do hope not. If only there was something one could do to help.'

He shrugged. 'That's a point on which I have to agree with Archie. The circus will be gone soon, and no doubt they'll be keen to put the memory of their time in Nuala behind them. We should do the same.'

'Did you find anything else of interest in Boris's quarters?'

'Comparing them with Alexei's, it's clear that he was the one in charge of the business side of the circus, but that was all.' As he'd decided that the pomade was not relevant, he didn't mention it.

They fell silent. De Silva gazed at the evening sky as its vivid colours dimmed with the onset of dusk. In the distance a line of birds, storks from the size of them, flew across it, their black silhouettes eventually fading from view.

'I suppose I had better report to Archie in the morning. Not that he has shown much interest in the matter.'

'You mustn't be too hard on him, dear. I'm sure he's preoccupied with the news from home and these jewel thefts. He and Florence still have friends and family back in Britain, and the outbreak of war must have been particularly alarming for anyone who remembers the last one.'

'True. I'm sorry.' He squeezed her hand. 'I'm sure it worries you too.'

'Yes. Even though I don't have ties to England now, it was my home for so long. But the situation is strange at present. People say millions of sandbags are being collected up and barrage balloons launched to force the German bomber planes to fly higher, but aside from that, nothing much has happened since war was declared. People are calling it the phoney war.'

'Maybe the Germans will make peace.'

'I doubt it,' said Jane with a sigh.

If the war didn't come to an early end, de Silva wondered how much it would touch their lives in Ceylon. He thought of Charlie Frobisher, training with the Royal Air Force, and felt a stab of apprehension. Should war come to this part of the world, he was bound to be at risk. And even if it did not, he might be sent home to fight in Europe.

He heard a meow and leant down to stroke Bella who was rubbing her head against his leg. 'Anyway, I hope we have no more climbing incidents with you.'

Jane laughed. 'Oh, I'm afraid we probably will. I think the pair of them are going to keep us on our toes.'

CHAPTER 10

The following morning, he was fishing in his pocket for the key to the police station when he heard a familiar voice greet him. Looking up, he saw Prasanna swing a leg over the saddle of his bicycle.

'You're early, Sergeant. Didn't I tell you and Nadar you needn't hurry?'

'You did, sir, but there's something I thought you would like to hear.'

'Oh? Well, let's go inside.'

Prasanna wheeled his bicycle to the side passage, chained it up and followed him indoors. Already sat at his desk, de Silva beckoned him into the office.

'I went to visit my mother yesterday evening, sir,' Prasanna began.

'I hope all is well with her.'

'It is, thank you. It was on the way home later in the evening that I saw what I want to tell you about. It was the snake charmer from the circus, Kumar.'

De Silva frowned. He wondered what business Kumar had in town. 'Where did you see him?'

'Near the bazaar. It seemed strange for him to be there at night, so I decided to follow him.'

'Did he see you?'

'I don't think so. I did my best to keep out of sight.'

'So, where did he go?'

As Prasanna explained about the part of town and the incident with the two men, de Silva picked up a pencil and scribbled a few notes on a pad. The area Prasanna described was one of the most unsavoury ones in Nuala. Why would Kumar want to go there even if, according to Prasanna's account, he was well able to look after himself?

'Did anyone else go into the house while you were watching?'

'No, sir.'

'Did you see him leave?'

'I didn't wait for that; sorry, sir. Perhaps I should have done, but it was getting late and Kuveni worries.'

'Never mind.'

After all, Prasanna had not been on duty. It would be unfair to reprimand him, although it would have been good to know more. He tapped his pencil against his teeth, debating how to proceed. 'Could you find your way back to the place?' he asked after a few moments.

'Yes, sir.'

'Then I'd like you to take me. Maybe we'll find out something about the owners and what goes on there. We'd better not draw attention to ourselves though. Go home and change out of your uniform. I'll wait for you here.'

* * *

While he waited for Prasanna to return, de Silva took off his own uniform and donned the plain clothes that he kept at the station. Twenty minutes later, Prasanna was back and they set off.

As they walked along, de Silva recognised some of the streets, although it had been a long time since he had visited this part of town.

'That's the one, sir.' Prasanna stopped and pointed to a house with a black front door.

'Stop waving your arms around, Sergeant. If anyone's looking, we don't want them to think we're interested in the place. Turn to face me, as if we're just two friends who have met in the street having a talk.'

'Sorry, sir.'

He glanced past Prasanna's shoulder. There was nothing exceptional about the house that particularly distinguished it from its neighbours. Like theirs, the paint on its door and windows was shabby; the few plants that grew against the wall straggled wearily from the ground. It was a pity there were no shops in the street. Sometimes a garrulous shop-keeper was a useful source of information. Knocking on the doors of any of the neighbouring houses was unwise. Apart from the fact that he didn't want to explain his interest, neighbours might tell the owner of the house that someone was making inquiries.

Searching for an idea, he noticed an old man trudging along the street. At the first house he came to, the man stopped and knocked, waiting a little while for the door to be answered. When it was not, he repeated the process at the next door. This time the door opened, and he spoke to the occupant for a few moments, but whatever he wanted was presumably not being granted, for he went on to the next house. He was, de Silva observed, respectably dressed in a clean sarong and tunic. Not a beggar then. Maybe he was selling something, but if so, the occupiers of the houses were not interested in examining his wares.

Eventually, after getting no answer at many of the doors, including the one he and Prasanna were interested in, the old man drew level with them and nodded a greeting.

De Silva smiled. 'Business bad today?'

With a grunt the old man shifted the pack on his back. 'I work all the streets around here. Usually this one is good, but today no one wants their knives grinding.'

'How often do you come along here?'

'Once a month, maybe. It depends how much work there is in other streets.'

'Do you see that house?' Surreptitiously, de Silva indicated it with a nod of his head.

'Yes, what about it?'

'Does anyone ever answer the door?'

'The last couple of times I've tried they do, but they've not given me any business. I wonder why I bother, sometimes.'

'What sort of people are they?'

'Tight-fisted people,' the old man replied. A laugh rumbled in his scrawny throat. 'Not from around here,' he added. 'Chinese.'

'Is it a man or a woman who answers the door?'

'A woman, but I have seen men in the background and heard their voices.'

Thanking him, de Silva gave him a few coins for the information. One never knew when he might be useful again.

'I think we'll come back tonight,' he said to Prasanna, as the old man disappeared into an adjoining street. 'Where did you watch from yesterday?'

'From behind that tree, sir.'

It was the only one in the street and the trunk was not wide. To be on the safe side, maybe he had better come alone. As they retraced their steps, he took careful note of the route. As he did so, he remembered when he had last been interested in the neighbourhood.

* * *

It had been not long after he came to take over in Nuala. The Colombo police had apprehended some members of the Black Lotus gang, the Hong Kong band of criminals who had been trying to extend their operations to Ceylon.

There was a rumour that they had a safe house in Nuala where they had stashed some of their loot. He had been given the job of identifying the place and leading some of his old Colombo colleagues to it, but if the gang had ever used the house he had identified, they had already left the area. His mission was a failure.

What interested him now was that the suspect property had been only a few streets from the house Kumar had visited the previous evening. Before he did anything else, he decided to speak to Inspector Singh at Hatton. The proximity of the houses and Kumar's visit might be mere coincidence, but it was surprising how often coincidences turned out to be more than that. Nothing in the crime reports had indicated that a reorganised Black Lotus gang were suspected of being behind the recent jewel thefts, but it was not beyond the bounds of possibility, and Singh might by now know more than the reports revealed.

He had told Prasanna to go home, and Nadar had not arrived yet, so he telephoned the Hatton station himself.

'How are you getting on with your circus case?' asked Singh.

'If you had asked me that question yesterday, I would have told you that everything has been resolved, and as far as the two deaths go, I think that's still true, but this morning, thanks to my sergeant, I became aware of a new angle.'

Singh listened while he explained about Kumar. 'Has there been any suggestion that the Black Lotus gang might be behind the theft at the de Vere plantation or any of the others?' he asked.

'I've spoken to Colombo several times,' said Singh. 'There are similarities in the cases, but no one has mentioned their name. Aren't they old history?'

'One would like to think so, and I agree the connection is speculative, but I'd like to follow it up.'

'I'll see what I can do from my end.'

'Excellent.'

'What do you know about this man Kumar?'

'Not a great deal. He didn't work for the circus when it was in Russia, as is the case with the majority of the members. He joined them in India, but he has travelled with them for some time.'

'Did he say where he joined them in India?'

'At the time, I didn't see any need to ask. He just mentioned that his family came from Madras. Kumar was friendly with the dead man, Alexei Goncharov, and his brother, who is now the sole owner of the business, appears to trust him. All the same, I'd like to know what he was doing visiting that house.'

'Has it occurred to you that your sergeant may have got the wrong man?'

'I think it's unlikely, but I hope to be able to verify that tonight.'

'Well, the best of luck to you. I look forward to hearing from you again. At least you have made some progress in your case. It's more than I can say.'

Was this progress, wondered de Silva as he put down the receiver. Or was it a dead end? Whatever turned out to be the case, it was probably time he reported to Archie Clutterbuck.

* * *

Archie was at work in his study, and the receptionist put de Silva through straight away.

'Good morning, de Silva.' Archie's voice had an edge of impatience to it. 'What have you got for me? I hope it won't take long. I have a meeting in ten minutes.'

'I'll try to be brief, sir.'

He heard a rumble of assent when he explained that Izabella had been released. Archie also sounded pleased to hear that the circus would not be staying in Nuala for too much longer.

'What about the couple who died?' he asked.

'Boris Goncharov wants them buried here. I had hoped to speak to Reverend Peters about it yesterday. I left a message with his wife, but he didn't call me back.'

'You'd better telephone him again. It's not for me to meddle in church affairs, but you might like to mention that I'd be grateful if the matter was dealt with, and with the minimum of fuss.'

'I will, sir.'

De Silva hesitated; he almost heard Archie looking at his watch, but he couldn't afford a delay.

'There's one more thing.'

'Yes?'

'My sergeant recognised one of the circus people, Kumar the snake charmer, in town yesterday evening. He was behaving as if he didn't want to be noticed. Prasanna followed him and thought he would have to go to his aid when Kumar was accosted by two men, but as it turned out, he was perfectly capable of defending himself.'

When he had described the incident in more detail as Prasanna had recounted it, Archie grunted approvingly. 'I'm glad to hear the ruffians got their comeuppance. What happened after that?'

'Kumar carried on to the rough part of town to the north of the bazaar and went into a house there.'

'Odd, I agree,' said Archie after a short pause. 'But there might be all kinds of reasons. We're aware there are gambling dens in that area, and for all we know, he might have been looking for female company, if you take my meaning. Do you have a particular reason for being interested in his activities?'

'I do; the house was close to one that I remember raiding many years ago. It was suspected of being a safe house for the Black Lotus gang.'

'Hmm. If I remember rightly, your part in eventually apprehending them was an early feather in your cap up here.'

'It's good of you to say so, sir.'

'But why that gang in particular?'

A local man who goes around the streets offering to sharpen knives told me the current occupants are Chinese. That's out of the ordinary in Nuala.'

'I suppose it is. So, I take it you're making the connection between them and the recent burglaries.'

'I believe it's an angle worth exploring.'

'What do you propose to do?'

'For a start, I want to watch the house this evening. If I'm lucky and Kumar returns, it would be interesting to know where he goes afterwards.'

'Well, by all means do as you propose. It would certainly increase our standing with the powers that be in Colombo if we managed to lead them to the criminals.'

From Archie's tone, de Silva was not sure that his boss was sanguine about the chances of that, but at least he had not dismissed the idea out of hand. He thanked him and rang off. Now all he had to do was pass the time until nightfall.

CHAPTER 11

'Hello, dear,' said Jane breaking off from the note she was writing in the drawing room. 'I wasn't expecting you back so early.'

De Silva went over and kissed her cheek then stroked Billy and Bella, who had come out from under the desk to greet him. 'I wasn't expecting it myself. I presume I'm too late for lunch.'

'I've eaten, but I'll tell cook to make something for you.'

'Anything light will be fine.'

Jane went to the mantelpiece and rang the bell to summon one of the servants. When they came, she gave orders for a light lunch to be served as soon as possible.

'I suppose it was quiet at the station this morning,' she said, returning to her desk. She signed the note, put it in an envelope with another piece of paper and started to write the address. 'I just want to finish this to catch the post. It's a knitting pattern I promised one of the ladies at the sewing circle.' She finished addressing the envelope and stamped it. 'There. Now you can tell me what Archie had to say about your letting Izabella go.'

'Oh, he was perfectly happy about it, and pleased to hear that the circus is likely to be leaving Nuala soon.'

'That's the end of the story, I suppose.'

'Maybe; maybe not.'

'You're sounding very mysterious, dear. Why do you say that?'

He explained about Prasanna's sighting of Kumar and what they had learnt that morning from the knife grinder.

'Did you tell Archie about it?'

'Yes. His reaction was not as dismissive as I thought it might be. He made the connection with the jewel thefts for himself and agreed it would be worth going back tonight in the hope that Kumar returns. But I doubt that he will support me in a further investigation if I draw a blank there. And I must admit, I'm not at all sure how I would proceed if that was the case. I've not much to go on, and as Archie said, Kumar might have had various reasons for visiting the house, gambling being one of them.'

'Is it possible to find out more about the place?'

'That's the problem; only by asking neighbours. And if whoever occupies it has criminal connections and gets wind that someone is asking, they will be off in two shakes of a sheep's tail.'

'A lamb's tail, dear.'

A servant appeared announcing that lunch was ready in the dining room. Sitting down to it, for a few minutes, de Silva concentrated on eating. 'Ah, that was good,' he said when he had polished off a plateful of vegetable and tofu curry with rice. 'I can think better now.'

Jane laughed. 'I'm sure cook would be flattered to hear it.'

He paused a moment, then helped himself to another spoonful of curry. 'But regrettably, my conclusion at present is that if Kumar doesn't show up tonight, I still have no idea what to do next.'

* * *

By the time he had finished lunch, there were still a few hours left until sunset. He wanted it to be dark when he went back to the house, so he decided to spend those hours at home. One of the servants brought tea and he and Jane drank it on the verandah. He had recently told Anif, their gardener, to replant some of the large pots there, and he admired the luxuriant ferns and oleanders the gardener had chosen. The sweet apricot fragrance of their deep-pink flowers was very pleasing.

'Will you take Prasanna with you this evening?' asked Jane.

He shook his head. 'If two of us are there, it might make it too obvious that the house is being watched. I'll go alone this time. That way, it will be easier to stay out of sight.'

Jane frowned. 'You will take care, won't you?'

'Of course.'

'Are you sure it wouldn't be safer to have Prasanna with you?'

'Absolutely sure. You mustn't worry.'

'I can't help it. If this is something to do with the Black Lotus gang, they are such violent people.'

De Silva stroked Bella who was sitting on his lap; she purred.

'Perhaps I should take you with me, oh vanquisher of crows,' he said with a smile. 'Seriously, I will be careful. I've not forgotten how dangerous the Black Lotus gang are.'

'You must wear old clothes so that you don't stand out. I'll look out something for you. I think I have a few of the servants' old clothes waiting to go to charity.'

'No need. I have a suitable sarong and shirt in the shed.'

Jane pulled a face. 'Not those dreadful tattered gardening clothes you won't let me throw away. You'll look like a tramp.'

He grinned. 'Isn't that what you want? They will fit the bill perfectly.'

Putting Bella down, he stood up. 'I think I'll take a walk around the garden while it's still light.'

In the vegetable garden, rows of runner beans flaunted scarlet flowers; bees buzzed in the herb garden where marjoram, thyme, rosemary, and sage were grown for use in the kitchen, as well as lavender for the muslin sachets that Jane liked to make to perfume drawers and cupboards. De Silva stopped briefly to enjoy the many scents then went on to the shed where tools and gardening equipment were kept.

The old clothes he was looking for hung on a peg by the door. He found a small sack and stuffed them into it then took a trowel from another hook and went outside. Bending down, he scooped a little earth into the sack. After that he tied it up, returned the trowel to its hook and walked around to the front of the house to put the sack in the Morris's boot. Dusting off his hands, he went back into the house to find Jane.

* * *

They ate supper early then he drove to the police station. There, he changed into the gardening clothes. At the last minute, Jane had provided a pair of worn-out sandals and he slipped them on.

The soil he'd collected had fallen to the bottom of the sack. In the washroom at the back of the station, he scooped some out and rubbed it on his legs, arms, and face, then looked in the mirror above the sink to gauge the effect. Some dirt in his hair would be a good idea too. After another handful, he studied his reflection again. Much better. It was a pity that he looked rather too well fed, but in a dark street he should pass for a man with no home to go to.

Leaving the Morris parked at the station, he set off for the house. The street was quiet when he reached it. He squatted down against the wall, close to Prasanna's tree, and began his vigil.

Time passed. A few people walked by, but they all ignored him. Sadly, he reflected that it was a taste of what life must be like for those unfortunate enough to live like this all the time. Eventually a few coins dropped on the ground beside him, and looking up, his eyes met the kindly ones of an elderly man. He muttered a thank you, not sure whether to be glad that his disguise was working or sorry that the elderly man's charity had been wrongly bestowed.

The moon rose, bathing the street in a wan light. Warmer lights glowed in the windows of some of the houses, including the one he hoped Kumar would visit. Through open windows, he heard conversation and laughter, enticing smells of cooking mingled with the odour of drains. Every time he heard footsteps he thought that it might be Kumar, but the hours went by and still there was no sign of him. No matter how many times he shifted position, de Silva's muscles ached ferociously. No longer enticing, the cooking smells were stale, and the odour of drains increasingly pungent.

At last, when he was almost ready to give up, a man walked into the street. He was the right height and build for Kumar. Tensing, de Silva watched him as he approached. He seemed to be in no hurry, stopping at one point to lean against a wall. A match flared, then the tip of a cigarette glowed in the darkness. The snatch of light had confirmed that it was definitely Kumar. He stood and smoked for a minute or two before throwing down the cigarette and grinding it out with his heel. De Silva guessed that he had paused to see if he was being followed. As he reached the Chinese house, Silva thought he would pass it by, but then he stopped. Briskly, he walked up the steps and knocked at the door. It was answered quickly, and he went inside.

The waiting resumed, but this time it was over much sooner. De Silva estimated that Kumar had been in the house for less than ten minutes when he emerged. Now, he had a small bag slung over his shoulder. De Silva waited for a few moments to give him a head start, then followed.

The road that Kumar took was the one leading to the racecourse. It took almost an hour to walk there. The walk loosened up de Silva's stiff muscles, but by the time the circus tents came into view his feet were sore, and a blister was coming up on the side of his big toe where the old sandal had rubbed it.

Once inside the racecourse, he hung back. If he followed Kumar's route over the open ground between the main buildings and the circus tents, the fellow only needed to glance back to see that he was being followed. He would also have to walk through the tented camp where, from the glow of small fires, people still appeared to be awake. Instead, he turned left along the course, planning to arrive at the back of the tented area. Hopefully, he would be in time to creep through and see where Kumar was going.

Luck was on his side. Kumar speedily covered the distance from the racecourse buildings to the tented camp but then slowed down to talk to some of the stayers-up who hailed him. Satisfied that he was far enough away not to be noticed, de Silva quickened his step and reached the back of the tent where Boris had his quarters. Nadia's tent was next to it; from it came the rhythmic sound of her snoring.

He was debating where to go next, when the faint sound of someone whistling attracted his attention. He remembered the tune; it had been the one Kumar had been whistling on Sunday afternoon when he found him shoeing the horse. The sound died, and de Silva grimaced. Kumar might have gone in another direction, or worse still, suspected he was being watched. Holding his breath, he edged forward then stopped abruptly whilst a dark figure crossed the narrow gap between the two tents. There was a soft sound of canvas moving as the flap of Nadia's was lifted.

Whoever had opened it, presumably Kumar, must have left it open allowing the moonlight to penetrate the interior, for de Silva detected movement inside the tent. As the intruder passed close to the place where he stood, with only the canvas wall separating them, he heard breathing – a muffled counterpoint to Nadia's stentorian tones. Soon, this new sound of breathing faded, and he could no longer be sure of the intruder's whereabouts. A slight breeze stirred the air. The canvas walls of the tents flapped sluggishly like the sails of a becalmed ship. De Silva counted the minutes and had reached three before he saw renewed movement, this time back towards the entrance to Nadia's tent. He heard the entrance flap close, then the rustle of footsteps on the coarse sandy grass. Counting another minute before he took the last few steps to the end of the gap, he peered out. There was no one in sight.

At the entrance to Nadia's tent, he listened for a few moments, then gently raised the flap and looked inside. The tent was in two sections, the first one being where Nadia slept. But in the darkness, it was impossible to see what the other was used for, and he didn't want to risk disturbing Nadia by going in further. Backing out, he let the flap down again. He suspected that Kumar had left whatever he had in that bag in the far section of Nadia's tent. Tomorrow, he needed to find a way of searching it.

* * *

Thoughts about how to deal with this development raced through his mind on the walk back to the police station. Only when he got there did he realise that the blister that had been coming up on his big toe was oozing watery blood. In the yard at the back, he used the outside tap to sluice the dirt from his arms and legs and put his head under it to rinse his hair. Coming up, he shook like a dog, spraying the ground. Next he washed his feet, flinching when he reached the blister, then went to sit on the bench over by a wall. The evening air would dry him soon enough.

Back in his office, he removed the old clothes and put on his clean ones. The mirror in the washroom showed that his hair was an unruly mess, but he was a lot more presentable than he had been half an hour ago. Now to drive home.

The house was quiet when he came into the hall. Billy and Bella raised their heads from their basket, their jade eyes blinking. He went over and stroked them then, slipping off his shoes, tiptoed to the drawing room. He felt too tense to sleep; perhaps a whisky would help.

The curtains were open and moonlight shone into the room. Going to the sideboard, he poured himself a generous whisky and went to sit in his chair to drink it. What had made it worth Kumar's while to walk into town two evenings running? If he had come out of the house with nothing, de Silva would have been tempted to accept one of Archie's theories, but the small bag the snake charmer carried inclined him to think otherwise. Even if he had gone to the house to gamble, surely he wouldn't have needed a bag to carry his winnings? Far more likely that he had gone to fetch something small, but valuable. Jewellery was an obvious deduction. Was he right in thinking that Kumar had a connection to the burglary at the de Vere plantation? And perhaps to some of the other jewellery thefts too?

The peaty warmth of the whisky relaxed him. He drank the last drop and wondered whether to have another one, but that would involve getting up from his chair, and the sideboard seemed a long way off. A cloud drifted over the moon, and the room darkened. His head felt heavy; his eyes closed.

CHAPTER 12

'Shanti! You should have come to bed, not slept in the chair. What time did you get home?'

Groggy with sleep, he saw Jane standing in front of him in her dressing gown. Outside, a tangerine sky showed that it was dawn. He flexed his stiff limbs and rubbed his eyes.

'And what have you done to your hair?'

'Give me a minute, and I'll explain.' He tried to stand but one leg was numb, and he sank back in his chair, rubbing the calf.

'Are you hurt?' asked Jane anxiously.

He shook his head. 'No, just stiff.' He explained about seeing Kumar and the walk to and from the racecourse.

'And then you slept in your chair – it's no wonder you're stiff,' said Jane. 'You must have a hot bath before you do anything else.'

'Good idea.'

In the bathroom, he eased himself into the deep bath that Jane had run for him and lay back with a sigh of relief. Jane perched herself on the bathroom stool.

'Thank you, this is just what I need,' he said with a smile.

'So, what did Kumar do when he got to the racecourse?'

'I'm a hundred per cent certain he went to Nadia's tent, but didn't wake her. When he came out, I suspect it was without whatever was in that bag I told you about. What other reason would he have to go in without waking her?

It might be that he let her sleep because he didn't need her help, but I think it's more likely it was because she's not involved in whatever he's up to and he needed a hiding place other than his own tent.'

'He was taking a risk. She might have woken.'

De Silva chuckled. 'If you'd heard her snoring, you might not think it was much of a risk.'

'Will you go back and search her tent today?'

'Yes, but I don't want her to know. Even if she is not involved, I've no idea how she will react. I want to know a lot more about what's going on before I reveal to anyone that I saw him.' He frowned. 'It might happen by chance, but if not, I'll need to think of a way of getting her out of her tent.' He ducked his head under the water and came up hair dripping. 'Any ideas?'

'What about Reverend Peters? Why not take him with you to talk to Boris about the funeral arrangements? I don't think it would arouse suspicion if you invited Nadia to join them. After all, she was close to both Tatiana and Alexei.'

'That's an excellent idea, but I'd rather he didn't know my motive.'

'Why does he need to?'

'I suppose he doesn't. And that reminds me, he still hasn't returned my call.'

'Then telephone him again. It can be your excuse that Boris is anxious to finalise everything, and you have time to take him up to the circus this morning.'

The bathwater sloshed against the side of tub as he stood up and reached for a towel.

'But the first thing you must do is have some breakfast,' said Jane firmly.

'That won't be a hardship.'

As he dried his feet, she noticed the blister. 'That needs some antiseptic and a bandage.' She went to fetch them, and he winced as the antiseptic stung. Jane applied a bandage.

'There, it will take a few days to get better, so no more long walks until it does.'

'I hope it won't be necessary.'

* * *

After breakfast, he telephoned the vicarage, and Reverend Peters came to the telephone.

'Ah, Inspector de Silva, my wife gave me your message. My apologies for not coming back to you sooner, but I wanted time to think the matter over.'

De Silva heard the vicar suck in his breath.

'It's a knotty problem,' Peters went on. 'Relations between us and the Orthodox church are cordial, and I hope there will be no problem with the young lady, but where Alexei Goncharov is concerned, it is a different matter. Strictly speaking, the church does not permit a funeral service and burial in consecrated ground when a person took their own life. However, I am aware that in a spirit of Christian charity and for the sake of the bereaved families, some of my brethren have, on occasion, obtained consent to depart from the official line. I'll see what can be done, but I will have to consult the diocesan authorities in Kandy. I'm afraid that at this stage, I'm unable to predict what the bishop's reaction will be.'

'I'm sure Boris Goncharov will be grateful for your kind efforts. I know he is eager to speak with you. There's also a lady called Nadia who looked after Alexei and Tatiana as well as Boris when they were children. Boris tells me she's like a member of the family. If you're able to accompany me, I have time this morning to take you up to the circus.'

'Well...' Peters sounded hesitant. 'It is more usual for the family to come to the vicarage.'

'On this occasion, I'd be grateful if you'd depart from your customary practice.'

'Why would that be?'

'If you don't mind, I'd rather not say.'

There was a short pause. 'Is the reason something that would trouble my conscience?' asked Peters at last.

De Silva considered the question for a moment. 'I believe not.'

'Then you need not tell me more. What time would you like me to be ready?'

'Would an hour be too soon?'

'Not at all. I'll be ready.'

* * *

On his arrival at the vicarage, de Silva rang the bell and waited, admiring the profusion of orchids that grew in large terracotta pots on either side of the front porch. He complimented Reverend Peters on them as they walked to the Morris.

'In England, growing tender plants in one's garden is impractical. Here, I have the pleasure of being able to do so to my heart's content. I have to admit, even though there are times when I miss the land of my birth, I wouldn't like to return to her cold, rainy winters.'

'Have you been away from England long?' asked de Silva. He had never engaged in more than the occasional bit of small talk with the vicar. Getting him to talk about himself should ensure that he didn't ask awkward questions.

'Almost twenty-five years.'

Only half listening to Peters' lengthy reminiscences about the places he had ministered in before being sent to Nuala, de Silva ran over in his mind how he was going to excuse himself from the discussion about the funeral. His thoughts dwelt too on the search he hoped to carry out. Unexpectedly, he felt slightly uncomfortable about it. He tried to analyse why and decided that what troubled him was the prospect of unearthing something that incriminated a man Boris Goncharov obviously trusted. Hadn't the ringmaster suffered enough? But then he quashed the feeling of distaste. If Kumar was involved in shady dealings, he had to be stopped.

When they reached the racecourse, they headed straight for the area where the circus was pitched. De Silva was relieved to see Gordo sitting by one of the tents. He immediately offered to take them to find Boris.

He was in the main tent, supervising operations to take it down. Dust drifted about as sweating circus hands rolled canvas into mountainous bundles and hauled them away to be put on the wagons. Loose wires rang against poles as other circus hands dismantled the tent's metal skeleton and tossed its constituent pieces onto clanging heaps. It was sad to see how ephemeral the magic of the circus was.

Directing the work with impatient shouts and gestures, Boris looked weary. 'We will go to my tent,' he said when de Silva explained why they had come. He beckoned to one of the older circus hands who was nearby and shouted something over the noise. Presumably, it was an instruction to take over. The man nodded.

As they walked to Boris's tent, de Silva suggested that Nadia should be included in the discussions. To his relief Boris accepted readily, and as they passed her tent, they collected her. At the entrance to Boris's own one, de Silva excused himself.

'I don't want to intrude,' he said. 'I'm sure you'd prefer to talk to Reverend Peters in private. I'll just walk around for a while.'

Boris thanked him and he, Nadia and Reverend Peters went into the tent. Waiting a few moments to make sure they were settled there and checking no one else was in view, de Silva pulled aside the entrance flap to Nadia's tent and slipped inside.

He had been concerned that any noise he made while he was searching might be noticed, but in daylight, he realised that the section he wanted to be in was adjacent to the sleeping area in Boris's tent. He would still need to be quiet, but there was less danger than he had feared of attracting attention. It worried him, however, that he might not have time for a thorough search before the meeting next door ended. There were more than twenty trunks to deal with. Fortunately they were not locked; indeed, some were opened.

The first dozen or so were packed with meticulously folded costumes. These included the folk dresses and oriental costumes that he had seen the dancers wear, as well as flamenco dresses in scarlet and black taffeta, matador costumes, the clowns' harlequin outfits, ballet tutus, and many others.

When he had done with the first trunks and found nothing untoward, de Silva went back to Nadia's bedroom and listened at the entrance to the tent. He heard the low murmur of voices from Boris's one. He, Nadia and Reverend Peters must still be talking. Returning to the trunks, he resumed his search.

The rest of the trunks contained wigs, shoes, hats, and a selection of elaborate headdresses, tiaras, and jewellery. As quietly as he could, he gingerly picked up a few pieces from the latter selection and studied them. On close inspection, the metal they were made of was thin and the gemstones were tawdry. It was obvious, even to his untrained eye, that they were paste. But a few of the pieces were a different matter. The gold looked genuine, and if the gemstones were fakes, they were very convincing ones.

He sat back on his haunches and looked around the tent. He had searched everything in it now. Had Kumar been carrying some of this jewellery when he left the club last night? And if so, who had he collected it from?

136

He re-examined one of the necklaces. It was of a distinctive design, but in some places, the rubies that should have been set into it were missing. He glanced at a jewelled band that looked like a hair ornament. There were rubies in that too. Was he imagining it, or was there a lack of uniformity in them? The depth of colour in some of the stones was closer to those in the necklace.

All at once, he remembered the glowing brazier and Kumar shoeing the horse. Hadn't he said his father was a blacksmith and had taught him the skills to work with metal? What if Kumar was using those skills to replace fake gemstones with genuine ones in the costume jewellery and accessories? It would be the perfect hiding place: not only a way of transporting them from where they had been stolen, but also of allowing them to be sold with far less danger of being found out. If necessary, the gold settings could be melted down and the jewels sold separately.

He considered the collection again. If he was onto something with Kumar, it was vital not to arouse his suspicions, but he needed an expert opinion on whether some of the jewels were genuine. There was a jeweller in town who had helped him before; his discretion could be relied upon. After a few moments' hesitation, he took a few rings, a brooch, the jewelled band, and the necklace.

With the haul tucked away in his pockets, he took out his notebook and wrote brief descriptions of the other pieces that interested him, then closed the trunk and eased the catches shut. It was fortunate that Nadia had not thought to lock it, but then why would she if she had no idea there was anything valuable inside? Cautiously, he returned once more to her sleeping quarters and listened at the entrance. Reverend Peters' tendency towards verbosity was another thing to be grateful for. The conversation had not ended yet.

Leaving the tent, he wandered off to a patch of open ground where there was a view over town. Nuala looked very peaceful in the sunshine, but he knew that in reality it would be bustling with all of its usual morning activities. The bazaar would be full of colour and shoppers; delivery trucks and cars would be hooting as they edged through the crowds; the perfumed smoke of incense would be drifting from flower-strewn roadside shrines; cows would be ambling through the streets, and stray dogs foraging.

'Good morning!'

He swung round to see Kumar smiling at him.

'Good morning to you.'

'Is there something I can help you with?'

Painfully aware of the jewellery in his pockets, de Silva then chided himself for being ridiculous. The man might have a way with snakes, but surely he didn't have the power to see through clothing. Still, he must take care.

'Thank you for the offer, but no. I'm only here because I drove our local vicar up to speak to your boss about the funeral arrangements for his brother and Tatiana.'

Kumar sighed. 'Of course. He and Nadia have been worried about what can be done.'

'I hope Reverend Peters will be able to set their minds at rest.'

'And once it is over, we will go. The circus loses money if we do no shows. More important, people need change to help them forget.'

And if you are what I think you are, thought de Silva, *you have another reason for wanting to shake the dust of Nuala off your feet*. He had better get the jewellery assessed as soon as possible.

He smiled, assuming a nonchalant tone. 'Has it been decided where you'll go?'

Did he imagine a flicker of wariness in Kumar's eyes? After a moment, the man shrugged. 'South, perhaps. After this tour, Alexei talked of going to Australia. Perhaps Boris will decide to go there.'

That would certainly put a safe distance between Kumar and the Ceylon police.

A voice called his name. He glanced over his shoulder and saw Reverend Peters coming across the grass.

'Ah, there you are, Inspector de Silva. Well, I've had a good talk with our Russian friends, and I think we have made some progress. I'll telephone the bishop's secretary when I get back to the vicarage and ask him to arrange for me to have a word with the bishop. I've warned Mr Goncharov we may have to wait several days for a decision. Now, if you're ready, shall we return to town?' He nodded to Kumar. 'A pleasure to see you again. I enjoyed our talk.'

'I too enjoyed it,' said Kumar with grave politeness. 'I do not meet many people with your knowledge of snakes.'

They sauntered towards the tents, conversing about the vicar's pet subject. It remained a mystery to de Silva how anyone found it so absorbing. Near to what remained of the main tent, they parted company, leaving Kumar to go about his business. On the drive back to town, Reverend Peters still dwelt on the subject of snakes. If he was curious as to whether de Silva's errand had been a success, he was too tactful to ask.

* * *

He left Peters at the vicarage and went on to the police station. Prasanna and Nadar were in the public room, bent industriously over their work. They both stood up.

'Anything to report?' he asked.

'A lady from Doctor Hebden's surgery telephoned earlier on, sir,' said Prasanna. 'She gave Doctor Hebden your message. He will meet you at twelve o'clock at the undertakers' office.'

De Silva clapped a hand to his forehead; he had forgotten

about the business of wanting Hebden to take a look at Alexei's body. He glanced at the clock. It was already ten minutes to twelve.

'We haven't telephoned to say you will not be coming, sir,' added Prasanna. 'I spoke to Mrs de Silva a little while ago, and she said we should wait to see if you were back in time.'

Briefly, de Silva considered calling, but Hebden was probably on his way. In any case, he would need to examine Alexei's body to make the medical report for the coroner. It wasn't far to the undertakers, and it would be more polite to explain in person that he no longer needed the advice he had thought he would and apologise if he had wasted Hebden's time.

'You did the right thing,' he said. 'I'll go round now and try to catch him. If he rings here, please tell him I'm on my way.'

After quickly stowing the jewellery in a bag and placing it in the safe in his office, he hurried out to the Morris. He realised that he hadn't told Prasanna how important his sighting of Kumar had turned out to be, but it would have to wait. He must be sure, however, to remember to praise him. It was an excellent thing that he was increasingly showing initiative. Nadar was a little further behind in that, although still a good worker. But one had to recognise that not everyone had it in them to advance to higher things, and the world needed its Nadars as well as its Prasannas.

It took longer than usual to reach the undertakers' premises, and it was twenty past twelve when he arrived. As he jumped out of the car, Hebden emerged.

'My apologies for keeping you waiting, Doctor Hebden.'

'Think nothing of it. I should have waited for you to confirm the time. In any case, you weren't keeping me from anything important. I only had a few appointments booked in this morning. My patients seem to have managed to stay healthy in my absence.'

'I'm pleased to hear it. I hope you enjoyed your fishing trip.'

'Very much; we had some excellent sport.' He gestured to the undertakers' premises. 'Do you need to go inside? If not, shall we talk out here?'

'Certainly.'

They strolled over to where there was a patch of shade close by where Hebden's car was parked. 'You said in your note that you would like me to examine Alexei Goncharov's body with a view to advising you on whether he might have been dead before the hanging,' he said. 'From that, I take it you suspect he might not have killed himself.'

'It's something I was considering,' said de Silva, 'but the situation has changed. I'm sorry if your time was wasted.'

'That's quite alright. I'm afraid that in any event, my expertise doesn't extend to giving you a definitive answer. It's not beyond the bounds of possibility, but I wouldn't like to stand up in court and swear it is what happened. A tragic business all round,' he went on. 'How is the brother taking it?'

'He seems to be bearing up, but I'm sure he'll be glad to move on and put Nuala behind him.'

Hebden nodded. 'Well, I'd better be on my way.' He looked at his watch. 'I have a few house calls to make this afternoon.'

De Silva thanked him and walked back to the Morris. His hand was on the door handle when Hebden called over to him.

'By the way, I forgot to mention something. It's probably unimportant, but I found a strange mark on Alexei Goncharov's right forearm. Two puncture wounds that nearly meet at one end so that it's shaped like a V. From the bruising around it, it must have been made shortly before he died. Do you have any idea what Goncharov was doing before then?'

'I know from his friend, Kumar, that they turned the horses out together early that morning, and he had an argument with his brother late the previous evening, but otherwise, I'm not sure.'

Hebden looked thoughtful. 'It certainly didn't look like anything a horse would do, and it seems unlikely that he caught it on a rough surface. I'd expect a wound from something like that to be a longer gash. If it were not so improbable, I would have said that the mark was caused by a snakebite.'

CHAPTER 13

As he drove home, de Silva's mind raced. Was it so improbable?

'It's been a most interesting morning,' he said to Jane as they ate lunch. He proceeded to tell her about the jewellery and other things he had found in the trunk at the circus and his theory that Kumar was working for the gang who had stolen it by hiding it and then moving it on for them. He went on to recount his conversation with Doctor Hebden and the mention of a snakebite.

'That certainly is interesting.'

'Yes. It seems too much of a coincidence that Alexei suffered a bite from a wild snake shortly before he died, so it's a reasonable conclusion that it was one of Kumar's. I doubt it was an accidental escape, and that suggests Kumar is not only an accessory to the de Vere jewellery theft and others, but also a murderer. If it is the case that Alexei was bitten before he was hung, it was probably to ensure that he was unable to struggle.'

'But would the snake's venom have acted on him quickly enough? I've always understood that if one is bitten by a snake, incapacity and death are not instantaneous. In fact, the process can be very slow and painful.'

De Silva shuddered at the thought. 'That's something on which I need expert advice, and I have the very man in mind.'

'Reverend Peters?'

'Yes.'

'Will you tell him why you want to know?'

'I may have to let him into part of the secret and ask him to keep it to himself for the moment.'

Jane frowned. 'How would Kumar have got Alexei close enough to the snake for it to bite him without his having time to save himself?'

De Silva remembered the picnic basket he had noticed in the stables.

'So,' said Jane thoughtfully when he told her about it. 'If Alexei wanted to avoid his brother because of their argument the previous evening, Kumar might have pretended he was being helpful bringing him food, so he didn't have to eat with the company, but what was really in the basket was a snake.'

'And when Alexei opened the lid, it would have been alarmed and reacted by attacking him.'

'But why would Kumar want to kill Alexei? And what about Tatiana?'

De Silva pondered for a while. 'Possibly Alexei found out what Kumar was up to and agreed to help him hide the jewellery and transport it from place to place in return for a cut of the profits. To start with, he might have been satisfied with a modest share, but what if he became greedy and wanted more? As co-owner of the circus, he might have thought that his position entitled him to demand it.'

'That might be the case. But where does Tatiana fit in?'

'Kumar may have engineered her accident, thinking that Alexei's alleged suicide would be more convincing if people believed he had intended her to die too.'

'Will you speak to Archie yet?'

'No. Before I do, I want to show the jewels that I took from that trunk to William Cradler, the jeweller. I want his opinion on whether they're fakes or not and I need to do that before Kumar notices they are missing. I'll call

Inspector Singh too. I wrote down descriptions of the pieces that I thought might be genuine. I hope he'll be able to tell me if my descriptions match any of the items stolen from the de Veres or any of the other families who were burgled.'

* * *

After lunch, de Silva retrieved the jewellery from the station safe and drove on to William Cradler's shop. He had always felt that there was something forbidding about the shop's exterior. The frames of its many-paned windows were painted black. The door was also black and the lintel lower than usual, so that unless a customer was short, they had to stoop as they entered. One also had to take care not to stumble on the low step just inside the threshold. On his occasional visits to buy a present for Jane, de Silva had felt as if he were entering the cottage of a wicked witch in a fairy tale.

A sepulchral-sounding bell clanged as he opened the door and went in. Of middle age, with greying hair and watery blue eyes behind pebble spectacles, William Cradler greeted him with a smile. Despite his shop's unnerving atmosphere, he was an amiable man.

'Good afternoon, Inspector. What can I do for you today?'

'I'm afraid I've not come to make a purchase. I'd like your advice on some pieces of jewellery I have with me.'

'By all means.'

Cradler put the silver bracelet that he had been polishing back in its velvet-lined box and tucked it away in a drawer. Producing a piece of green baize, he unrolled it on the glass-topped counter. 'Lay them out here if you will.'

De Silva placed his collection on the counter. Cradler switched on the electric lamp at his elbow, picked up one of the rings and studied it. The light from the lamp caught the stones, making them sparkle.

'Are the diamonds genuine?' asked de Silva. Cradler examined them with a magnifying glass. 'Yes.' He took another ring. 'These are too. How did you come by them?'

'I'd prefer not to say, and I'd be obliged if you would treat my visit as confidential.'

Cradler nodded. 'I understand.' He put down the rings. 'I estimate their value would be somewhere in the region of one hundred pounds each. Now, this necklace is a more interesting piece. It's a pity that some of the rubies are missing. It reduces the value considerably. I may be able to replace them if you wish, but the quality of the existing ones is very high. It would be an expensive business.'

'I don't need them replacing, but I would be interested to know what you think of the rubies in this.' De Silva indicated the headband.

The jeweller picked it up and studied the stones. 'Strange,' he mused. 'Most of these are paste, but I'm convinced a few are genuine rubies.' He held the headdress out to de Silva. 'Do you see how the colour differs?'

He put down the headband. 'Why anyone chose to set them in a cheap piece of tin is a mystery to me, but no doubt it makes sense to you.'

After Cradler had looked over the remaining pieces and given his opinion that they were genuine, de Silva thanked him and returned to the Morris. The jeweller had certainly given him plenty to think about.

At the station, he placed the jewellery in his office safe, locked it, and pocketed the key. His next job was to telephone Inspector Singh at Hatton.

* * *

When he came on the line, Singh didn't sound his usual unruffled self. 'I'm afraid I can't talk for long,' he said. 'I need to return the call that Mr de Vere made while I was out this morning. He's extremely impatient over the lack of success we are having with recovering his wife's jewellery. I don't want to make things any worse than they already are.'

'I'm sorry to hear of your difficulties, but I hope to be able to help.'

Singh listened, occasionally intervening to ask a question, as de Silva recounted the recent events involving Kumar. He recognised several of the pieces that de Silva described.

'They match what the de Veres say they lost, but would you send me descriptions of everything you've found?' he asked.

'With pleasure.'

'I'll find out more from the Kandy force about what has gone missing down there, but I assume you'd rather I didn't pass on everything you've told me quite yet.'

'I would.'

A deep chuckle rumbled from Singh's throat. 'Better to have your man in custody before the Kandy boys start crawling all over the place, eh?'

De Silva laughed. 'No disrespect to our esteemed colleagues, but they do have a habit of thinking that we provincial policemen ought to stand back and leave them to get on with the job. I'll send the details down this evening and keep you informed, my friend.'

'Do you propose to put a watch on the house in case the occupants try to leave? There may be more stolen items in their possession, and it would be a feather in our caps if we apprehend them, particularly if they're connected to the Black Lotus gang.'

'It's too risky to send my sergeant. Kumar has seen him several times now. If he comes back to the house and spots him, there's a real danger it will give the game away. My constable would be a safer bet, but he may need some help.'

'No problem. I'll send you some of my people to keep an eye on the house with him. If they come by car, they'll have transport to follow the occupants if they need to. I may not be able to arrange it before tomorrow, however.'

'Thank you. That should do fine.'

Ending the call, de Silva went into the public room and told Nadar what had been arranged. His eyes lit up at the prospect. He was obviously happy at the idea of taking a more active part in the case than minding the cantankerous Izabella Rabach.

'You had better hold the fort here,' he said to Prasanna.

'Yes, sir.' Prasanna sounded a little disconsolate.

De Silva grinned. 'Cheer up, Sergeant. It looks like your sighting of Kumar the evening before last may prove to be a turning point in the case.'

Prasanna's expression brightened.

'But there isn't time to go into all that now,' de Silva added. 'I have another job for you both that needs doing straight away.'

He gave them the notes on the jewellery that he had made at the circus. 'I want those copying out as quickly as you can and sent to Inspector Singh at Hatton. Drop them at the post office on your way home. I don't expect anything more to happen this evening, but make sure you are here on time tomorrow.'

Back in his office, de Silva deliberated whether to make a call to Archie. A lot had happened since he had last updated him, but was this the right time? He felt the same hesitancy as he had towards involving the Kandy police. If Archie knew there was a chance of recovering the de Veres' jewels, and possibly those belonging to other members of the British community, he would, for sure, want to mount a raid. It might be extremely difficult to persuade him to hold back on the grounds that closing the case on Alexei and Tatiana had possibly been a mistake.

As he considered what the best course of action would be, a fat bluebottle bumped against the window, then dropped to the sill, its spidery legs twitching. The ceiling fan rotated with its usual monotonous thrum. At last, he decided not to telephone Archie. Until Alexei's and Tatiana's funeral had taken place, the circus wouldn't be going anywhere, and while the circus remained in town, so would Kumar. Hopefully, he would not feel the need to check on the whereabouts of the jewellery de Siva had removed.

What de Siva did want, however, was to hear Jane's opinion on the afternoon's developments. Going to the safe, he took out the jewellery. She would enjoy seeing it.

* * *

Before going home, he drove to a spot some way off from the house that Nadar and the Hatton reinforcements would be watching in the morning. He wanted to satisfy himself that nothing had changed, and that in leaving its occupants alone he was not being rash. Parking the Morris, he walked the rest of the way, arriving at the place where he had waited the night before last. The sun had already sunk below the line of the rooftops. The yellow glow of lights picked out the windows of some of the houses, but not the house he was interested in. For a moment he feared he was already too late, but then the front door opened. He tensed and shrank back into the shadows, but it was only an old woman with a bucket of water that she tipped down a nearby drain. She went back into the house and closed the door. Shortly afterwards, a light went on in one of the downstairs windows.

The scene looked so peaceful and domestic. It was hard

to credit that members of a gang as justly feared and violent as the Black Lotus lived in the house. But wasn't that the secret of their success? He remembered from his Colombo days how cleverly the brains behind the operation had selected agents who blended in with the run of ordinary people. They were also ingenious in the way they constructed their chain of command; whenever you thought you had reached the apex of the pyramid your hopes were invariably dashed. It had taken years of painstaking work to flush out the branch of the organisation that operated in Ceylon. Gloom filled him when he thought of how much work might be required in order to do so again.

* * *

It was dusk when he reached Sunnybank, and a familiar little shadow greeted him by the front door. He scooped her up and she purred. Jane was just coming into the hall from the drawing room.

'Ah, there she is. She seems to have a sixth sense for when you arrive home. We were in the garden until a few minutes ago, then she suddenly ran off.'

'She's a clever girl.' He put Bella down. 'I'll go and change.'

'You do that, dear. The three of us will be waiting on the verandah to hear your news.'

Dressed in cooler, more comfortable clothes, de Silva went to the sideboard in the drawing room and poured himself a whisky. The soda from the siphon fizzed into the tumbler with a satisfying sound.

'Shall I bring you out a sherry?' he called to Jane.

'Yes, please.'

On the verandah, he put the drinks on the low table between their chairs and sat down.

'How did your visit to William Cradler go?'

'I think you would call it a success.'

He produced the jewellery and arranged the pieces on the table. Jane picked up the headband.

'This is very exotic. It looks like one of the ones the dancers at the circus wore in their performance. But surely, it's not valuable, is it? It's far more likely to be costume jewellery.'

'Cradler's opinion was that some of the stones in it are genuine.' He explained his theory about Kumar substituting real for fake stones as a means of concealing them.

'I agree that would be an ingenious way of doing it,' said Jane.

'If there was a danger of any of the pieces of jewellery being identified, the stones could be removed from their setting once again and sold piecemeal.'

Jane nodded. 'And the gold melted down and sold separately too.'

'Do you think that makes sense?'

'I do.'

'I telephoned Singh when I got back to the station. He was glad to hear what I had to tell him. The poor fellow is under a lot of pressure to find the jewellery stolen from the de Veres.'

'Did he think any of these pieces belonged to them?'

'Not these in particular, but he reckoned some of the ones I described do. I told Prasanna and Nadar to copy out the list and get it in the evening post. It should be with him in the morning. He'll compare it with the information he has from the de Veres. Also, he'll find out more about the rest of the jewellery that's gone missing over the last few months.'

'Wouldn't it be marvellous if you've found everything.'

'That might be too much to hope for.'

'Have you told anyone else?'

'Not yet.'

He explained his reservations about Archie, and she nodded. 'I see what you mean, but I wouldn't leave it too long.'

'Oh, I don't intend to. I want to talk to Reverend Peters in the morning. I hope that he'll provide me with the piece in the puzzle that gives me enough evidence to arrest Kumar.'

Deep in thought, Jane stroked Billy, who sat on her lap. 'Does it strike you as very convenient that some of Alexei's horses were lame that day?' she asked after a few moments. 'Without that, there would have been no valid reason for him not to perform his act.'

'That's a very good point. Since your friend George Appleby is a vet, he might be able to throw some light on it for us. I'll try to speak to him as well as Reverend Peters in the morning.'

CHAPTER 14

It was Charlotte Appleby who came to the telephone when he called the following morning.

'I'm afraid my husband has already left for the surgery,' she said. 'If you ring there in about twenty minutes, you should catch him before he goes out on his rounds.'

De Silva thanked her and tried the vicarage, but Reverend Peters was also unavailable. 'He went over to the church straight after breakfast,' said Mrs Peters, 'and he has some visits to make after that; but I expect him home for lunch. He plans to spend the afternoon working on his sermon. Would it be convenient for you to come at about two o'clock?'

He confirmed that it would and went back to tell Jane.

'I'll have another cup of tea then telephone Appleby's surgery.'

'Are you worried about having to wait to speak to the vicar?' Jane poured tea into their cups from the pretty, rose-patterned teapot. Fragrant steam drifted towards him.

De Silva shook his head. 'I know the main tent is already down and they haven't much left to do, but I think we can be confident Boris won't take the circus off until after the funerals. In any case, it may be best to go up later. If I get there when Kumar is helping to bring in the horses from grazing and settle them for the night, I should be able to search his quarters uninterrupted. Otherwise, I may have to take Boris into my confidence and ask him to find a way of keeping Kumar out of the way, but I'd far rather avoid that for the moment. Not because I think he is involved in Kumar's crimes, but because his reaction may be violent and difficult to contain.'

A vision of Boris grabbing Kumar by the throat and trying to shake the truth out of him rose before his eyes. He looked at his watch and drank the last of his tea. 'I'll go and call Appleby, then I'd better be off to the station. The reinforcements from Hatton should be up here soon.'

George Appleby's receptionist put him straight through and he heard the veterinary surgeon's calm, professional voice at the other end of the line.

'Is this about those kittens of yours, Inspector? Your wife mentioned that you might like a word about the operations that I suggested they have.'

'I would like that at some point, sir, but it's not the reason I'm calling you today. This may seem a strange question, and I must ask if you wouldn't mention to anyone that I've asked it, but I'd be grateful for your help.'

'You intrigue me. Go on.'

'It concerns horses. What I need to know is whether it's possible to lame a horse on purpose.'

'That is an unusual question, and something I hope you have no intention of trying, but yes, it can be done. An easy way would be to remove one of the animal's shoes and hammer a stone or some other hard object into the soft part of the hoof.'

Immediately, de Silva's thoughts flashed back to the afternoon when he had seen Kumar shoeing one of Alexei's horses. Had he been removing a stone he had previously inserted in the hoof to make the horse lame? He thanked Appleby, grateful for the traditional British reserve that made it easy not to let slip more information than one had intended.

'What did he say?' asked Jane when he returned to the dining room.

'It's easily done, and I think I may have seen Kumar reversing the process.' He described what Appleby had told him.

'Those poor horses. And the wicked man professes to be fond of them.'

'At least for them, unlike for Tatiana and Alexei, the damage was curable.' He looked at his watch. 'It's time I was off to the station.'

Jane's forehead creased. 'You will be careful, won't you? This man Kumar seems very dangerous.'

He put his arm around her shoulders and bent down to kiss her cheek. 'I promise not to do anything foolhardy. A man who's as much at home with snakes as this Kumar is not an adversary I intend to treat lightly.'

'But there are these jewel thieves too and probably the Black Lotus gang.'

'Perhaps, but I've dealt with the gang before. You mustn't worry. I won't take any risks.'

Jane gave him a rueful smile. 'How many times have you promised me that?'

* * *

He had just finished bringing Prasanna and Nadar up to date with everything that had happened when Inspector Singh's men arrived.

'You'd better come into my office,' he said when they had introduced themselves. 'You too, Nadar.'

In contrast to Prasanna and Nadar, the Hatton sergeant was plump, and it was the constable who was tall with an athletic build. As de Silva had instructed Nadar to be, they were both dressed in everyday clothes in order not to stand out while they performed their task. Observing their earnest young faces, de Silva felt a sudden awareness of his age. He wondered whether, as a young man, he had looked as nervous when presented with a new superior. There had certainly been occasions when he had felt it.

'Any questions?' he asked when he had explained that he wanted them to watch the house and take note of any comings and goings.

'If someone leaves the house, should we follow them, sir?' asked the sergeant.

'Provided you can do so without being noticed. I'll have to leave that to your discretion.'

'What if they all seem to be leaving, sir?' asked Nadar.

'Then you should definitely follow them. But I hope that won't be a situation you have to deal with. Now, you'd better get off. Nadar, show them the way, please.'

After the three of them had gone, de Silva settled down to talk to Prasanna.

'I hope you understand that it's no reflection on your work that I've sent Nadar rather than you,' he said. 'It's just that if Kumar happens to come back to the house at any time, he may recognise you as he's seen you several times.'

'That's alright, sir.'

Prasanna looked thoughtful. 'Sir, I've been wondering—' He paused.

'Yes?'

'If Kumar is a murderer as well as being in league with the jewel thieves, do you think Boris Goncharov might be at risk too?'

'What makes you say that?'

'I was just thinking of what you said about the circus being owned jointly by the brothers. If Kumar killed them both, it would give him the chance to try and take complete control. He might like the idea of that. If he's working for the jewel thieves, he could dictate wherever the circus went to suit them.'

'Hmm. That would be presuming Kumar can prove he is entitled to inherit.'

'Or he thinks that no one will question him if he claims that is the case,' said Prasanna eagerly.

'An interesting theory, Prasanna. Well done. I'll bear it in mind, but I'd like to have some concrete proof to back it up.'

He looked at his watch. 'I have a couple of hours before I'm due at the vicarage to talk to Reverend Peters about snakes.' A shiver went through him. 'How do you feel about snakes, Sergeant?'

'Mostly they are harmless, sir, if you leave them alone. There was one in the washhouse for our building a few weeks ago. Some of the men wanted to kill it, but I managed to trap it in a bag and set it free where it would do no harm.'

'Very laudable. Well, I think it's time we had lunch.' He fished in his pocket for some money and handed it over. 'Please go to the bazaar and get enough for us both.'

As Prasanna departed on his errand, de Silva reflected that the young man often surprised him. He might be the ideal companion for this trip to the circus. When he returned with lunch, he would talk to him about it. And even if his help wasn't needed with the snakes, it seemed unfair to exclude him when he had made such a valuable contribution to the case.

CHAPTER 15

The vicarage's mellow stone walls basked in the afternoon sunshine. As if to remind viewers of its inhabitant's calling, the tall windows were set in pointed Gothic arches decorated with carvings that were more modest versions of those at the church that stood not far away. A vigorous soft-pink rose spread its branches between the windows, also scrambling over the roof of the deep entrance porch. The latter was floored with tiles decorated with a fleur-de-lis pattern of faded blue on a yellowish-cream glaze, well-worn by many years of footsteps; the front door was a massive piece of oak.

De Silva tugged on the brass bell pull and heard a jangling sound from inside the house. He waited a few long moments and was wondering whether to ring again when a servant answered the door.

'I believe Reverend Peters is expecting me.'

The servant nodded. 'Please come in, sahib. I will let him know you are here.'

The narrow window in the entrance hall didn't allow much light to penetrate, and with its dark-stained panelling, the space had a gloomy air. Under the window there was a heavy oak table with bulbous legs; on it were a salver for letters and a pretty blue and white jug containing red roses.

He had only been waiting a few moments when Mrs Peters came to greet him. 'I'm afraid we've only just finished lunch,' she said apologetically. 'My husband's appointments ran late this morning. Will you join us for some tea in the garden?'

'With pleasure, ma'am.'

Mrs Peters turned to the servant who was hovering in the background. 'Please bring out another cup and a fresh pot of tea.'

Unlike Sunnybank, which was built in the traditional style of colonial bungalows, the vicarage didn't have a verandah. Instead, there was a stone-flagged terrace. Decorative metal chairs with seat cushions covered in floral cretonne were arranged around a metal table; a large parasol in the same fabric provided shade. More climbing roses covered the rear of the house and roses filled many of the flowerbeds. Others contained oleander, hibiscus, lilies, and in the shadier spots, ferns. Pink, yellow, and cream waterlilies covered the surface of a small pond. The picturesque scene, with its profusion of colours and scents, delighted de Silva. He recalled from a previous visit that beyond the garden, there was a glasshouse where the Reverend Peters kept his prized collection of orchids.

Peters rose from his seat and shook de Silva's hand. 'We meet again,' he said with a smile. 'I've managed to have a word with the bishop's secretary to explain the situation. He will speak with the bishop and come back to me in the next few days.'

'Thank you.'

'A pleasure. Now, what can I do for you?'

The same servant appeared carrying a tray with the tea.

'Let the inspector drink his tea in peace before you start questioning him, dear,' said Mrs Peters. 'Do you take your tea black, Inspector?'

'I do, thank you, ma'am.'

Her husband pushed his cup across the table. 'I'll have another one too.'

'What a charming garden this is,' remarked de Silva as he accepted his cup of tea. 'It must give you a great deal of pleasure.'

'Indeed it does,' said Peters. 'But I believe you are an enthusiast too, and your own garden is a fine one. If you have time, I'd be delighted to show you the orchid house before you go. My Kandyan Dancer is flowering for the first time, and I have an interesting example of a rare monkey orchid that I grew from seed.'

They chatted about plants for a while as small, vividly coloured birds flitted about in the trees, butterflies hovered among the flowers, and iridescent blue and green dragon-flies skimmed the pond. When the tea had been drunk, Mrs Peters stood up. 'Well, I'll leave you gentlemen to discuss whatever brought the inspector here.' She rang the little brass bell beside her cup to summon a servant to clear the tea things.

'Shall we go to my study, Inspector?' asked Peters. 'The heat builds up in the afternoons, and I find it cooler and more comfortable there.'

'Certainly.'

The study was furnished with two windows that were both larger than the one in the hall; consequently, the room was slightly less gloomy, but also much more cluttered. De Silva wondered if Mrs Peters or any of the servants were ever allowed in to tidy it. Bookshelves overflowed, and there were letters and papers on every surface. As in the hall, the walls that were not fitted with shelving were covered with dark panelling, and the built-in wooden seats under the windows were also made of dark wood. Two easy chairs covered in claret-coloured velvet that matched the curtains stood on either side of the fireplace. Reverend Peters was right, the room was pleasantly cool, even though it lacked a ceiling fan. The muted light coming through the windows indicated to de Silva that it faced north. There was a faint aroma of peppermints in the air. De Silva recalled that the vicar was not a smoker, but he was addicted to the pungent sweets.

'Am I right in thinking that your visit has something to do with the business at the circus?' he asked.

'Yes, but before I continue, may I have your assurance that this conversation will go no further?'

'That's not a problem. In my line of work, one is accustomed to respecting confidences.'

De Silva smiled. 'Thank you. I have no conclusive proof as yet, but the fact is, I believe there's a strong possibility that Alexei Goncharov did not commit suicide.'

Peters frowned. 'Do you mean he may have been murdered?'

'Yes.'

'You need not tell me who your suspects are.'

Nevertheless, Reverend Peters listened carefully while de Silva launched into the story of the jewellery thefts and Kumar's involvement. 'What I hope you can tell me,' he ended, 'is whether there is a snake so venomous that its bite would immediately paralyse or even kill its victim. There was no sign of a struggle before Alexei's death, and the only marks on his body, apart from the ones made by the rope, were the two small puncture wounds that Doctor Hebden spotted.'

Peters nodded. 'I understand. If there is no such snake, it makes your theory hard to credit.'

He stood up, went to one of his bookshelves and took down a thick volume. Leafing through the pages, he found the place he wanted then brought the book over to de Silva and placed it in front of him.

'I expect you'll be pleased to know that there is one.' He smiled. 'My wife tolerates my fascination with orchids, but she has always been adamant that she will never permit me to have a collection of live snakes. The illustration on the page in front of you is, however, faithful to the very few examples of this particular species that I have, in the past, seen in the wild and also, rather to my surprise, much more recently in the collection of your Mr Kumar. It is called the blue coral.'

De Silva studied the colour plate that showed a snake with a striking electric-blue body and a neon-red head and tail. Despite his aversion to snakes, he had to admit that the creature was extremely beautiful.

'Why do you say you were surprised?' he asked.

'Because the blue coral is one of the most dangerous snakes in the world. All snake venom kills by slowing down the victim's vital systems until they drift away into death. All the same, dangerous as a snakebite is, in most cases it requires some time to reach that point, so there is a reasonable chance of administering an antidote where there is one available. In the case of the blue coral, however, the venom sack is about a quarter the length of its body and extremely powerful. It has the effect of making all the nerves fire at once, causing violent convulsions. Paralysis of the whole body is swift and soon followed by death.'

De Silva felt his skin creep. With an effort, he composed himself as the vicar continued, a very non-ecclesiastical note of relish in his voice. 'In short, the blue coral is a killer's killer. It seeks its prey amongst other dangerous reptiles, including young king cobras and highly poisonous frogs. As I said, I was surprised to find it in Kumar's collection. Using it in his show would be dangerous to the point of foolhardiness. But when I asked him why he owned it, he told me it was out of fascination for the species, not with any intention of using it in any of his acts. A fascination I entirely understood.'

If Alexei Goncharov had been attacked by a blue coral, thought de Silva, it would be an understandable mistake to assume that any signs of convulsions on his dead body had been caused by the hanging.

'How likely would this blue coral be to attack a man?' he asked.

Peters shrugged. 'No more likely than most other snakes. In fact, it prefers to avoid humans, but if alarmed, like any snake, it will strike. What makes it so dangerous, of course, is the fact that if it does feel threatened and attacks, its bite is inevitably deadly.'

De Silva imagined the scene: Alexei opening the lid of the basket and reaching in for what he thought would be a tasty lunch, but instead finding something cold and scaly writhing under his fingers; its fangs piercing his skin; the poison flooding into his bloodstream... He shuddered.

'Agonising pain shoots through the victim's body,' Peters went on. 'Shock, delirium, terror, and swiftly, death.' He glanced at de Silva with an apologetic expression. 'Forgive me. My wife often tells me that I allow my enthusiasm to run away with me.'

De Silva felt a film of sweat coat his face; his uniform shirt had grown damp. He was in complete agreement with Mrs Peters, but the vicar was to be applauded for providing exactly the information he required.

'If the snake had been allowed to escape,' he said, 'what do you think the chances of Kumar recapturing it would have been?'

'Slim. As I said, the blue coral is shy of people. Its overriding desire would have been to escape as quickly as possible. In any case, I believe that even the most confident snake handler would be satisfied with one successful operation and baulk at risking their life on a second attempt at capture.'

'And if the snake did escape, where would it go?'

'By now, I expect it would be somewhere in the jungle. Even if it had spent a considerable portion of its life in captivity, the instinct to return to the wild remains strong in most creatures.'

A wave of relief washed over de Silva. He was glad to think that he was unlikely to meet it roaming free up at the circus.

'Is there anything else I can do for you?'

Closing the book, de Silva handed it back. 'Not at present, but many thanks. Your help has been invaluable.'

'Then I'll bid you goodbye. Of course, if your theory about Alexei Goncharov's death is right, it changes the position regarding his burial. But for the moment, would you still like me to speak with the bishop?'

In the excitement, de Silva had almost forgotten the issue of the funeral. His mind was already on the next thing that he needed to do, and as soon as possible: search Kumar's quarters, and also his collection of snakes. The thought of the latter task made his blood run cold. But if he turned out to be on the wrong track, a decision about the funeral would still need to be made. He could always step in to delay the service if necessary.

'I'd be obliged if you would and let me know the result.'

'Very well.' Peters smiled. 'I suggested showing you my orchid house before you leave, but I see that you have more urgent matters on your mind. Another time, perhaps.'

De Silva thanked him and returned to the police station.

CHAPTER 16

By the time he reached the station, it was almost four o'clock. If he and Prasanna left for the circus now, it was possible they'd arrive before Kumar had started to bring the horses in and settle them for the night, which would mean he might still be in his tent. Best to wait a while before setting off.

There was a lingering aroma of curry in the public room; the sounds of the street drifted in through the open window. Prasanna, who looked to have been daydreaming, sprang to attention, hastily fastening the top button of his tunic.

'Well, that was an extremely useful trip,' said de Silva, pretending not to notice his sergeant's disarray. 'I have a pretty good idea of what kind of snake we are looking for now. It's called a blue coral. An extremely beautiful creature. Have you ever seen one?'

'I don't think so, sir.'

De Silva described it, not leaving out the details of its deadly habits. 'You don't seem particularly alarmed, Sergeant,' he said when he reached the end.

'I'm not, sir. Since you say that Reverend Peters is an expert on snakes, and he says it will probably be in the jungle by now, I don't think there's any need to be.'

De Silva admired his optimism; he hoped it was not going to turn out to be misplaced. He consulted his watch. A leisurely drive before the ordeal might have a calming effect on his nerves.

'If we set off in half an hour,' he said, 'it should get us to the circus a little after five o'clock. With luck, it will be the perfect time to find Kumar safely out of the way. I hope we can find his tent without attracting attention.'

'It won't be hard, sir. It was pointed out to me when I was going around with Gordo.'

'Ah yes, you told me, and I had forgotten. Incidentally, did you find out anything else about Kumar at that time?'

Prasanna pondered for a moment. 'I remember that quite a few people seemed not to like him. I think there was something about him carrying on as if he was part of the management, just because he was a friend of Alexei's. I'm afraid I didn't follow it up though.'

'That alright. At the time, there was no reason why you would have thought it important.'

De Silva wondered whether another reason for Kumar's unpopularity might be that the Russians didn't like to see an Indian doing well, but whether that was the case or not, the information was interesting.

* * *

Inside the entrance to the racecourse, de Silva did his best to park the Morris in an inconspicuous place. He waited there while Prasanna went over to the stable yard to see if Kumar was about.

'There are several horses tethered in the yard, sir,' he said when he returned. 'And I heard noises from inside. I wanted to be sure it was Kumar, so I chanced a look around the door. He's on his own.'

'Well done. We'd better get a move on before he finishes his work. Don't forget, if anyone asks why we're here, we've come with a message from Reverend Peters for Boris. Once I get into Kumar's tent, you keep watch outside. Should you think anyone's coming, alert me, then melt into the background as fast as you can.'

They struck out across the course, Prasanna leading the way. The slanting, late afternoon sun threw bands of dark shadow and deep gold across the grass. With the circus's main tent gone, the sea of small ones looked forlorn. De Silva was relieved that not many of their inhabitants were about. Doubtless, now that the major packing up of the circus was done, and there were no shows until the circus's next stop, there was not much work for the circus hands or the performers. An air of lassitude hung over the place, as if in their minds, the circus people had already moved on from Nuala.

'We'll approach it from the back,' he muttered to Prasanna when they reached Kumar's tent. 'I may need you to slip through a gap for me and remove a flap of canvas so I can get in.'

Apparently unobserved, they reached the tent and found a suitable place at the back. Prasanna just managed to squeeze inside. The canvas billowed and creaked as, laboriously, he partially freed a section from its fastenings and peeled it back.

'Is the gap wide enough, sir?' he asked, poking his head out.

De Silva gave a low chuckle. 'I'm not as stout as all that, Sergeant.'

'Sorry, sir.' Prasanna grinned.

'Any sign of those snakes?'

Glancing around the tent, Prasanna shook his head. 'But there are a few photographs of him with them.'

'Maybe they're already on one of the trucks, ready for when the circus moves on. Out you come, and I'll get on with my search.'

Prasanna stepped through the gap and stood aside to let de Silva in. He was glad to see that there was not much in the tent. Searching it should be a reasonably quick job, which was a good thing in the circumstances. Apart from a bed, two canvas chairs and a washstand, there were just a couple of trunks. He started on the first one, taking care to replace the contents as he found them but uncovered nothing out of the ordinary. After he had closed the catch on the second one with the same result, he turned his attention to the bed. The sheets were made of thin cotton with a woollen blanket that felt slightly waxy to the touch laid over them. As he turned it back, he smelled a faint odour of lanolin. Pulling off the sheets, he shook them out, but nothing of interest was hidden there either. He also checked inside the pillowcase and felt the pillow for any suspicious lumps and bumps.

Next, he ran a hand between the mattress and the base of the bed. There was a crackling sound as he felt around, and he let out a muffled curse. Something sharp had jabbed his hand. Gingerly, he removed it and saw beads of blood that oozed until they became a rivulet. A yellowish-brown splinter had embedded itself in his skin. The mattress must be stuffed with straw and have a hole in the ticking. Carefully, he removed the splinter, causing more blood to flow. Alarmed, he noticed that some of it was on one of the sheets. He took his handkerchief out of his pocket, wrapped it around his bleeding hand and knotted it, then remade the bed as carefully as he could. Luckily, he was able to tuck the bloodstained part of the sheet out of sight beneath the mattress.

Just as he had finished, the sound of voices close to the entrance to the tent made him start; his heartbeat quickened. He must leave before it was too late. With a final glance at the bed to satisfy himself it looked near enough to how he had found it, he hurried to the gap in the canvas. It would be frustrating if Kumar had come back. He would have liked more time to search, so he might have to enlist Boris's help after all.

Outside, he pulled the canvas back into position as best as he could then waited, praying that no one would come around the corner and find him. Interspersed with laughter, the voices drifted towards him on the sultry air, but he was unable to make out what they were saying.

At last, the conversation died, and he was debating whether it was safe to go into the tent again when he saw a hand emerge through the gap. His throat went dry and he recoiled, catching his foot in a guy rope and stumbling. As he regained his balance, the gap widened. A familiar face appeared.

'For goodness' sake, Sergeant! You nearly gave me a heart attack.'

'Sorry, sir.'

'Was it you who was talking just now?'

Prasanna nodded. 'Gordo came past and struck up a conversation. I gave him the excuse you told me to and said I was strolling around while I waited for you. I didn't want to make him suspicious by trying to get rid of him too quickly. Shall I go back and keep watch again?'

'Yes, I haven't found anything so far. I want a bit more time.'

Back inside, he began to study the photographs. One of them showed a turbaned Kumar, dressed in trousers and tunic made of exotic brocade, with a snake draped over his shoulders for all the world as if it were a scarf.

He studied Kumar's dark, glittering eyes, and his enigmatic smile. What secrets lay behind them, and where was the evidence that would unlock those secrets? A feeling of frustration grew; he had a good chance of proving that Kumar was tied up with the jewellery thefts, but he was sure there was more to his crimes than that. At the moment though, establishing that he was responsible for the deaths of either or both of Tatiana and Alexei seemed a daunting hill to climb. Gloomily, he faced the prospect of his hunch leading nowhere.

At least his hand had stopped stinging. Untying the knot that secured the handkerchief, he found that the blood had clotted. He cast a final glance around the tent. It was a pity that apart from the photographs, the few pieces of furniture, and his clothes, Kumar seemed to have no possessions. He had hoped for papers or letters; something that would throw light on a link to a gang of jewel thieves, perhaps as he suspected, the Black Lotus gang. Had everything been done by word of mouth? Surely, there had been times when written messages were necessary. It would be feasible to send letters for Kumar to pick up at post offices in towns that the circus was going to visit, but if that was ever the case, he must have destroyed them.

Then an idea came to him: the mattress. He had been too preoccupied with his injured hand to search it thoroughly. What if the hole was big enough to slip papers or letters between the straw and the ticking? It would be a simple solution to the problem of how to conceal such things.

He didn't want another injury, so he cautiously lifted the mattress and peered underneath; the straw crackled in protest. It was not until he had raised it as high as his strength would allow that he saw the tear. It was several inches wide. Straining to hold the mattress up with one hand, he prodded the grubby, striped ticking around it. More straw spilled out, but he was sure there was something else in there. His arm ached from the weight of the mattress, but with an extra burst of effort, he pushed it higher and reached in with his free hand. He touched something smooth. Carefully, he eased it out and found it was a small pouch made of soft leather.

Lowering the mattress back in place, he tidied the bedding once again then turned his attention to the pouch. There were no letters, but what it did contain was much more interesting. Unfolding the document, he saw that it was an agreement between Kumar and Alexei, written in English and dated a few months previously. It referred to gambling debts and stipulated that if by a certain date Alexei had not repaid a large sum of money that he owed to Kumar for helping him out with them, his share in the circus would become the snake charmer's property. So, if Kumar was a gambler, as Archie had suggested, he was a successful one. It was Alexei who had been losing more than he could afford. A jolt went through de Silva as he read the repayment date. It was only a week away.

The truth came to him in a rush. Kumar hadn't killed Alexei because he was an accomplice in thieving whose presence had become inconvenient; he had killed him because time was running out for repayment of the loan. He was afraid that as the date approached and Alexei didn't repay, he would lose his nerve and appeal to Boris for help. The fact that he hadn't already done so was probably due to what Nadia had said about their father's wishes. No doubt Alexei had been hanging on for as long as possible, hoping for a miracle, rather than face his brother and admit what he had done. The consequences would almost certainly have been disastrous for Kumar too. Boris seemed to be an honourable man; no doubt, if the money was due, he would repay it, but Kumar's career in the circus would be over.

So, realistically, Kumar was faced with a choice between giving Alexei more time to pay or taking over his share in the circus and, for the time being at least, keeping quiet about it. But what good would that do him? Money? Admittedly he would be able to extract more from Alexei, but Prasanna had suggested, and it seemed plausible, that Kumar might want total control of the circus to enable him to take it to the places that best suited the jewel thieves. How would that be possible if he had to work through Alexei? Boris appeared to be the stronger character and would surely have the last word on destinations.

Suddenly, everything became clear. If the plan was to

work, Kumar would also need to get rid of Boris. And best of all, do it quickly, so that he could take control while the circus was already reeling from the loss of Alexei and Tatiana. Kumar must have some fate in mind for Boris, which, like Tatiana's "accident" and Alexei's "suicide" did not point the finger immediately at himself. De Silva stuffed the agreement in his pocket, but returned the leather pouch to its hiding place, then hurried out of the tent.

Outside, darkness was rapidly extinguishing a blood-red sky. He went to the corner and called to Prasanna in a low, urgent voice.

'Did you find anything, sir?' his sergeant asked.

'Yes. We need to find Boris as soon as possible. I believe his life is in danger.'

* * *

Boris wasn't in his tent, and he was not with Nadia either.

'I'll come back,' said de Silva. 'If you see him, tell him to wait here for me. I have something I need to speak to him about as soon as possible.'

Nadia looked bemused, but she nodded.

'We'd better keep moving,' he muttered to Prasanna. 'The racecourse is a big area. We may not have much time left to find him before it's too late. We'll try the tented camp. Perhaps he's talking with some of the circus people there.'

At the camp, small fires had already been lit. Firelight bathed the faces of the people sitting around them, throwing their features into eerily sharp relief. The cooks had already served up the evening meal, and mostly in silence, people were eating. As de Silva and Prasanna circled the camp, hostile eyes watched them over the rims of bowls of food. One man gave them a sour look as he gnawed the last

174

shreds of greasy meat from a chicken bone then tossed it into his fire.

They had reached the edge of the camp when a genial voice at his elbow made de Silva swing around.

'Good evening. You need help?' Gordo grinned at them. At least someone didn't regard them as unwelcome interlopers.

'We're looking for Boris,' said de Silva hastily. 'Do you have any idea where he is?'

'Maybe at the stables. I saw him walking in that direction earlier.'

A chill ran down de Silva's spine. 'What about Kumar?'

Gordo shrugged. 'Sorry, I do not know.'

He frowned as Prasanna pushed past him and broke into a run. 'Hey! What is hurry?'

De Silva grabbed his arm and jerked him around. 'No time to explain. Just come with us.'

* * *

Beyond the light of the campfires, only starlight showed the way. Tussocks of grass snatched at de Silva's feet as he ran, and specks of red and green danced before his eyes. His lungs felt ready to burst. As the stable area came closer, he smelled smoke. Racing into the yard, he saw Prasanna disappear into the office building where they had found Alexei's body.

The first room was filled with black smoke, and it was hard to see through it, but he heard blows and managed to make out that Prasanna was kicking at the door to the room at the far end. It gave way, and a wave of heat rolled out accompanied by an even denser cloud of smoke. Prasanna was already inside; de Silva's eyes streamed as he crossed the threshold after him, pulling up the lapel of his jacket to cover as much of his face as possible, and trying to hold his breath. Papers and straw looked to have been liberally scattered around. Much of it was already ablaze. His foot knocked against something, and he saw that it was a lantern lying on its side. The smell of oil was so powerful that he was sure it was a stronger one than would be made by the fuel from a single lantern.

Prasanna was backing towards the door, dragging a man by the feet. De Silva hurried to help him and realised that it was Boris. Between them, they hauled him out to the yard. De Silva straightened up and gulped a lungful of air. It was like nectar to his parched throat. 'Let's get him onto the grass. Gordo, find some water.' The clown, who had been standing by helplessly, rallied and hurried away.

De Silva glanced at the office building. The fire was rapidly taking hold. Even standing at the distance they were, the heat was hard to bear. From the barn where the horses were stabled, he heard terrified neighing. They were probably smelling the smoke. He didn't think there was much hope of saving the barn itself, but the horses needed to be got out before the fire spread.

Boris groaned as they laid him on the grass. It was a wonder they had been in time to save him. Fortunately his clothes, stinking of smoke as they were, had not caught fire. His guardian angel must have been watching over him, thought de Silva. He remembered the empty vodka bottles he had found at Boris's tent and the argument between him and Nadia he had overheard. He strongly suspected now that Kumar had put them there, paving the way for the story that a drunken Boris, grieving for his brother, had accidentally set light to the room where Alexei had been found hanged. He shuddered, thinking of the terrible end the snake charmer might have planned for his boss.

Boris's eyelids flickered, and briefly his eyes opened, the whites startling in his soot-blackened face. Feebly, he lifted a hand, and de Silva winced to see how badly blistered the skin was. Perhaps he had tried to crawl to safety, only to find the door locked.

'I'll look after him now,' he said. 'Hurry and send some people down here to help. We must get the horses out of the barn and try to contain the fire. Prasanna, once you've organised that, take Gordo and a couple of men and look for Kumar. When you find him, arrest him.'

'Shall I send someone to fetch the fire truck?' asked Prasanna.

'Good idea, but I hope someone will spot the blaze from town and send it up anyway.'

As Prasanna and Gordo hurried off, he propped Boris up with one arm and held to his cracked lips the cup of water that Gordo had brought. 'Try to drink a little of this,' he said.

Boris did so, but the fit of retching and coughing that ensued took a few moments to subside. 'The horses,' he croaked at last. 'Get the horses out.'

'Don't worry, I have people coming to deal with that. Can you tell me what happened?'

'Kumar…' Hoarsely, Boris forced the word out, but then another coughing fit robbed him of what little voice he had. Clearly, it was too soon to get him to talk.

'We'll catch him. Don't you worry,' he said soothingly. 'Save your voice now. You can tell me everything later.'

* * *

It wasn't long before a group of men from the circus arrived. Some of them led the terrified horses to safety and calmed them, while others removed all the combustible items that could be moved from the open barn between the office building and the main barn. Everything they had to leave behind was then liberally doused with water. It was fortunate, thought de Silva, that many years ago someone had decided to dig a well, so that the racecourse always had a good supply of water. It was too late for the office building, but the other two had a good chance of survival.

By the time Prasanna and Gordo returned with the handcuffed but struggling Kumar, Boris had recovered sufficiently to be able to sit up.

Kumar's face was a mask of fury. 'Why have I been arrested?' he snarled. 'I demand to be released immediately. I need to go to the horses and calm them.'

De Silva raised an eyebrow. 'The horses are being cared for, and I believe you know why you've been arrested.'

'If you think I had anything to do with this fire, you're crazy.' Kumar twisted in Prasanna's and Gordo's grip and lashed out with one foot, catching Gordo on the shin.

'Try that again, and I make sure you are lame for life,' growled the clown.

Kumar spat on the floor, and de Silva scowled. 'Take him to that gate over there. Gag him if you have to and shackle him to its bars. I'll drive back to town with Boris and leave him with Doctor Hebden. I also want to contact Inspector Singh and tell him that I think we have one of his villains, but once I've done that, I'll be back.' He turned to Prasanna. 'I'm leaving you in charge. Don't take any risks but keep on damping down the barns and their contents if you can.'

'Yes, sir.'

He helped Boris into the car and headed back to town. On the way, they passed the fire truck heading at speed for the racecourse, its bell clanging. Either the message had got there, or as he had hoped, the blaze had been spotted from town. That was good. With the firemen to take charge, there was a better chance that the remaining buildings would survive.

Calling first at the Hebdens' house, he left Boris in David Hebden's care and asked Emerald to telephone Jane to reassure her that he was safe. After that, he drove on to the station and telephoned Inspector Singh. The conversation lasted for several minutes then, satisfied that he could do no more in that direction, de Silva decided to return to the racecourse to supervise Kumar's transfer to the police station. He was halfway to the Morris when he realised that he had not reported events to Archie. Hurriedly, he went back inside and placed a call to the Residence. Fortunately, Archie had finished dinner and de Silva's report was well-received.

* * *

Much later that evening, he was at last able to telephone Jane.

'I'm so glad Emerald called me, or I would have been worried. How is Boris?'

'I've only had a brief word with Hebden since I left Boris with him, but he was fairly confident that it wouldn't take him too long to recover from the effects of the smoke he inhaled, although the burns will take longer to heal. From his account of what he remembers, we think Kumar must have hit him on the head then locked him in the back office, but again, Hebden doesn't think there will be any lasting damage.'

'Thank goodness. What a lucky escape he's had.'

'He certainly has.'

'Is the fire put out?'

'Yes. The circus people did a good job of saving the horses and stopping it from spreading. When the fire truck arrived, the firemen did the rest, although all that's left of the office building is a blackened ruin. The Royal Nuala

Jockey Club won't be pleased, but the important thing is that no lives were lost.'

'Emerald said Kumar has been arrested.'

'Yes, I have him in custody here. I'll stay tonight and keep an eye on him. Singh came up from Hatton earlier. He and his men, along with Prasanna and Nadar, raided the house that Kumar collected the jewellery from and made a number of arrests. I wanted to get on with that straight away in case the occupants got wind there was something up and made a run for it. Singh took them down to Hatton. I expect they'll soon be transferred to Kandy or Colombo for further questioning, as will Kumar. There are also details of the investigation to be completed, for example how he managed to tamper with the high wire without being spotted. I assume it was when the tent was deserted at lunchtime on the Saturday, but I expect Kandy will want everything thoroughly investigated.'

'Do you think they'll be able to prove that the people from the house are part of the Black Lotus gang?'

'I'd like to think so, but we mustn't get ahead of ourselves. Anyway, that will be someone else's job.'

'What an evil man Kumar is.'

'Indeed.'

'Those poor horses – they might have died horribly, and so might poor Boris Goncharov.'

'Unless Kumar intended to return and save them. But I imagine his plan was to leave it until it was too late to rescue Boris from the office building, by which time the barn might very well have been ablaze.'

'If no one stays in Nuala to be questioned, it may mean the case is taken away from you.'

'It almost certainly will be.'

'Do you mind?'

'Not really. We'll have gathered all the evidence we are likely to find about the murders so, although those were the worst of Kumar's crimes, the immediate focus will change to the jewel thefts and who else was involved. To be fair, none of the thefts occurred in Nuala. That doesn't lessen the credit we can take for catching a double murderer and for saving his next victim, Boris. And obviously, I will have to give evidence at Kumar's trial, which is likely to take place in Colombo.'

'You're being very reasonable about it, dear.'

He laughed. 'I'm a very reasonable man.'

CHAPTER 17

The congregation for Alexei's and Tatiana's funeral filled the church. Not only did all the circus folk attend, but there were also quite a few local people.

'I'm glad Archie and Florence came to pay their respects,' whispered Jane to de Silva. 'The Hebdens are here too.'

He and Jane had wondered what form the service would take. The funeral of two Russian Orthodox Christians in an Anglican church was an unusual event to say the least. However, Reverend Peters had managed successfully to adapt the official line, and the service was a beautiful one.

Doctor Hebden had advised against Boris attending, but he had refused point blank to stay away. Heavily bandaged, he made his way to his pew supported by two of the sturdiest circus hands.

Standing in for him, Gordo had spoken the eulogy, and as a tribute on behalf of the town, Archie gave the reading from the Bible. Listening to his gravelly tones, de Silva thought how well he rose to the occasion, his voice bringing out the majesty of the text.

After the final hymn, everyone filed out into the churchyard for the burial. The plots that had been chosen were in a peaceful spot under a tree in one corner. Now that it was clear that Alexei was a murder victim rather than having committed suicide, the religious objection no longer applied. With the sun warming his back as he stood with head bowed amongst the other mourners, de Silva hoped that Alexei's and Tatiana's souls would rest in peace.

'Boris asked Emerald if she would visit the graves sometimes,' said Jane as, with the burial service concluded, people began to move away. 'It may be a long time, if ever, before he returns to Nuala. I've said I'll help her. It would be nice to bring flowers.'

'That would be kind.'

Still needing support, Boris stood to one side of the path, accepting condolences as people paused to speak with him. De Silva admired his stoicism. Very likely, he remained in considerable pain.

Nadia stood to his right and Izabella Rabach to his left. 'She doesn't seem at all ferocious today,' whispered Jane after she and de Silva had offered their sympathies and moved on.

'Yes, she was surprisingly gracious.'

'Perhaps the tragedy has brought out a gentler side to her nature. Let's hope it lasts. Boris will need kindness.'

Outside the lychgate, the Hebdens fell into step with them. 'Goodness, I shall be glad to get out of this dress when we get home,' said Emerald. 'I had to wear it because it's the only black one I have.'

'But, Emerald, you never put on—' Jane stopped, her eyes widening.

Emerald giggled. 'Yes, I'm expecting a baby.'

'Oh, that's lovely news. I'm so happy for you both. When is it due?'

'Not until March. You're the first people we've told.'

'We're honoured,' said de Silva with a smile. 'Congratulations.'

They walked over to where their cars were parked. Solicitously, Hebden opened the passenger door and helped Emerald into her seat. She gave him a mischievous smile. 'I'm not an invalid, you know.'

'I know, but can't I make a fuss of my wife?'

'Of course you can.'

Jane smiled as the couple drove away. 'I'm so pleased for them.'

How life changed, thought de Silva. David Hebden had been such a stiff, formal man when he had first come into contact with him. Now he was happily married and soon to be a father.

The last stragglers from the congregation were getting into cars and circus trucks or walking away down the church path that led to town. De Silva saw Reverend Peters coming from the direction of the church porch, his black cassock billowing in the gentle breeze that had got up. He was glad he had got to know him a little better; Peters was a good, kind man. The funeral he had devised in the face of an unusual situation had been a moving one. According to Jane, it must have taken considerably more time and trouble than he usually expended on his services. To de Silva, it was proof that if anything had the power to unite different religions, it was kindness.

'You're looking pensive, dear,' said Jane. 'What are you thinking about?'

'Kindness, and how important it is.'

'It was certainly kind of Reverend Peters to take so much trouble over the service. I'm sure it was appreciated. Oh look, he's coming this way. Perhaps we should wait and congratulate him.'

'That's an excellent idea,' said de Silva, rubbing his hands.

'You seem particularly enthusiastic.' Jane looked at him with curiosity.

He chuckled. 'Last time he and I met, we talked about gardens, and he offered to show me the orchid house at the vicarage. I was in a hurry to leave, so I didn't take up the offer, but with luck, he'll extend the invitation again, and now I have time to accept it. It sounds like he has some interesting specimens.'

Jane tucked her arm into his and smiled. 'If necessary, I shall drop hints to make sure he does ask you. After everything that's happened, I think you deserve a treat.'

'It was all in the line of duty, my love. But thank you.'

Author's Note

Thank you so much for reading this book, I hope you enjoyed it. You can find details of my other books on my website or my blog and can also sign up from my blog to receive my monthly email newsletter which gives news of promotions, events, and new releases.

https://harrietsteel.com/
http://harrietsteel.blogspot.co.uk/.
Facebook Harriet Steel Author
Twitter @harrietsteel1

Printed in Great Britain
by Amazon